CONVERGENCE

THREE WORLDS, ONE LONG AFTERNOON

a novel

WILLIAM F. HARTMAN

TERRI L. HARTMAN

iUniverse, Inc.
New York Bloomington

Convergence: Three Worlds, One Long Afternoon

iUniverse books may be ordered through booksellers or by contacting:

iUniverse
1663 Liberty Drive
Bloomington, IN 47403
www.iuniverse.com
1-800-Authors (1-800-288-4677)

Because of the dynamic nature of the Internet, any Web addresses or links contained in this book may have changed since publication and may no longer be valid. The views expressed in this work are solely those of the author and do not necessarily reflect the views of the publisher, and the publisher hereby disclaims any responsibility for them.

ISBN: 978-1-4502-6067-1 (sc)
ISBN: 978-1-4502-6068-8 (dj)
ISBN: 978-1-4502-6069-5 (ebook)

Printed in the United States of America

iUniverse rev. date: 10/11/2010

To Jean, wife (WFH) and mother (TLH)

ACKNOWLEDGMENTS

Writing this book has not only been very enjoyable for me, it has also led to some unexpected gratification. All fathers remember the family council where everyone exhibited great enthusiasm for an upcoming family project only to discover, when the time for implementation arrived, only Dad was available to make it happen. This endeavor has proven to be the exact inverse. My daughter Terri, after a few words questioning her father's literary competency, volunteered to act as co-author with the hope of making it readable. Son Jon, in addition to accepting the responsibility for the illustrations and a marketing plan, claimed neither of us knew anything about grammar or punctuation; we suspect that he was right. Then my son-in-law, Doc Farnsworth, volunteered to design a cover for the book.

Through all of this, my wife Jean graciously persevered. I need to thank her and also all of my friends who, by now, are undoubtedly tired of hearing about Bill's damned book.

INTRODUCTION

Many books have been written that discuss various aspects of nuclear terrorism; few, if any, delve into the processes that would be required to defeat (or at least mitigate) a terrorist's nuclear device once it has been located. Such attempts will be exceedingly difficult and, quite possibly, may prove unsuccessful. I felt it important to call attention to the many points of view which must be reconciled to bring such an event to a proper culmination and to suggest that there is a realistic likelihood that the efforts to defeat the weapon will not be successful.

The events that are portrayed in this fictional situation are representative of those that might have occurred prior to 1995. Since that time, the technical response processes and procedures have been greatly improved but the extremely difficult problem of achieving consensus regarding the most favorable response activities in such a high-risk, emotional, time-constrained environment will always be situationaly-dependent.

There is, however, always one very basic condition that must be realized: failure to reach a timely decision is tantamount to making a decision.

PROLOGUE

It may look like boasting—but what I tell you is the truth—I began to reflect how magnificent a thing it was to die in this manner, and how foolish it was in me to think of so paltry a consideration of my own individual life, in view of so wonderful a manifestation of God's power.

Edgar Allen Poe,
A Descent Into the Maelstrom

Few men are anxious to die. Even for the first-hand observation of God's awesome power. That was certainly the case for the six men huddled and waiting that September afternoon in 1995 in the Parisian catacombs. They, Bison and his team of two other Americans and three Frenchmen, had already been sitting there way too long, waiting for the people upstairs to make a decision about if and how to disable the rogue nuclear artillery shell with which they were frighteningly sharing their underground cavern.

PART ONE

Three Worlds

CHAPTER ONE
Bison

His parents named him Bryson. Bryson Baird. As with many three year olds, there was something about the letter r that defied pronunciation. So when the grinning three-foot tall Bryson Baird would introduce himself to someone he didn't know, it would come out, "Hi, I'm Bison Baihd." So Bison it became, through grade school, through high school, through college, and into his professional life—always Bison. It was Bryson only to his mother and generally then only on those frequent occasions when she was displeased with him. Few people even knew his last name: Bison—or more familiarly, Bise—was enough. Even some of his professional colleagues later in life paused for a moment when someone mentioned Dr. Baird.

Growing up in a small upper-Midwest town in America in the 1940s and '50s, the son of a schoolteacher and a one-time high school football coach-turned-school-superintendent, Bison had as idyllic a childhood as it was possible to have. His world was straightforward and God-fearing: everyone was good until proven otherwise, a person's word was his or her bond, and everyone in your hometown was naturally your friend.

Tall and rangy, with unruly dark hair and horn rims he seemed to wear from birth, Bison possessed a mischievous smile that appeared to say, "Go ahead, just dare me." His impishness and natural charm meant he was spoiled by the town's elderly women, who always seemed to find a piece of candy in their purses when they spied "that rascal Bison" coming down the street.

Bison's parents were a little more suspicious of their son's cheeky nature. His mom, in particular, felt that it was somewhat inappropriate for the school superintendent's family to be anything but beyond reproach. To that end, she devoted herself to community work, serving happily as volunteer librarian and substitute high school teacher and less happily as president of the Women's

Christian Temperance Union (a group even she found too sanctimonious). Bison's dad was equally involved in the life of the town, attending school events three or four nights a week and devoting the rest of his spare time to the Masons and Shriners and acting as deacon and tending the church furnace on Sundays during the South Dakota winter.

Under their mother's watchful eye, Bison and his siblings were also active members of the community, either helping with their parents' activities or busy with jobs of their own. Throughout high school, Bison crammed in twelve to fifteen hours a week at the local newspaper office. He took great pride in his ability to compose stories right on the Linotype; it was only later that he realized these stories read exactly as if they were written as they were being set in type—completely without benefit of an editor or proofreader.

The hours spent working and in community service were enjoyable and made his folks happy, but to Bise they were utterly inconsequential. There was never any doubt in his mind that he would become a professional athlete. He spent hours, day after day, kicking a football through the ramshackle goal posts that he and his buddies erected on the lot between the parsonage and the Baptist church. If no one else could be recruited to play, he pushed a little dirt around the ball so it would stand up and then ran up and kicked it toward the goal post with the garage as a backstop. He would cheer as if it was a game-winner and then go fetch the ball and repeat the process. When this grew old, he would swing the tire attached to the overhang on the garage, stand back twenty yards, and try to spiral the ball through the moving target.

During his first week at state college, it became apparent that Bise's professional athletic career was not going to be a reality. His sparse body had finally started to fill out, but he still weighed less than two hundred pounds. The college football players were not only bigger, they had more talent and commitment. Bise wistfully gave up his dream and decided to just have a good time.

That plan worked, until his father called him aside the morning he packed his car to return to school for his junior year.

"So what do you think you'll do when you graduate, Bise? You'd better start thinking about it."

"Well, I haven't thought about it much, but maybe I'll become a coach like you did. That seems to have worked well for you."

"Like hell you will," his dad roared.

That got Bise's attention. His father would repeatedly admonish that "the use of profanity shows a person doesn't have a very good vocabulary," so for him to swear meant he felt strongly about the matter. Later in life, Bison's mother told him that his dad had always regretted not becoming an engineer and did not want his only son to have similar regrets by simply choosing the easy way out.

So, with his dreams of gridiron glory squashed, Bison went back to school that fall and became a somewhat reluctant engineering physics major. He quickly developed a comfortable rapport with Dr. Ford who, with his fatherly manner, would almost daily reproach Bison for his lack of commitment to his education and, in particular, to the optics class Dr. Ford was teaching. Almost every week Dr. Ford suggested special problems for Bison to tackle in the lab, problems that would "bring your grade up to a respectable level." Bison resisted until it got close to the end of the semester, and it became apparent that some extra credit was a necessity rather than a luxury.

One Friday night, having failed at both finding a date and talking his friends into doing something fun, he dragged himself to the Engineering building to tackle Dr. Ford's current special problem. All by himself in the dark, creaky old building, Bison fell in love with the process of scientific inquiry. He raced home at 3:00 am, overwhelmed with the excitement of discovery and eager to share this discovery with his roommates. When awakened, not one of them was at all interested in his newfound joy about the wave nature of light.

College suddenly offered a lot more value for Bison. He found the library. He enrolled in advanced ROTC. When someone asked about this decision, Bison's stock answer was, "I'll probably be drafted when I graduate and I'd rather be an officer," but in reality the $1.20 a day ROTC stipend was the deciding factor.

After four years, Bison graduated with a military commission and a GPA that elicited a "you could have done better" from his father. Bise didn't care: it had been a happy four years, and he was a graduate engineer at a time when engineers were much in demand.

The Army Chemical Corps beckoned. When Bise found himself in Alabama in July, completely wrapped in a rubber suit, boots, and gas mask, watching the effects of nerve gas on sheep, he had some serious doubts about the wisdom of his ROTC decision.

Then came Maryland. "Getting assigned to Maryland was one of the best things that ever happened to me," Bison was fond of telling anyone who would listen. "If I'd gone to some intriguing place like France or Japan, I wouldn't have met Bev."

The tall blonde met him (another oft-told, frequently embellished tale) in the lobby of the Personnel Building so she could escort him to the major, who was waiting to hear why Bise was late reporting for his duty assignment. Once Bise explained the misunderstanding to the major, he set about a far more serious task: finding out about the blonde. In an act of bravery that was completely out of character—he'd always been shy and intimated around women—he asked her out that very evening. He was taken not only by her cute butt and her tall, slender build but by her quick retorts to what he considered his droll verbal banter.

Either in spite of the banter or because of it, the couple wed the following summer. At the end of Bison's two-year service commitment, the job market for young engineers and scientists was very good. After considering various options, the newlyweds found themselves in Albuquerque in the late 1950s.

Albuquerque had not been an easy sell to Bev. "You want to go where?" she cried when he first told her about the job offer from the national nuclear weapons laboratory. She had been a terrific sport, though, and Albuquerque had been a good choice. Their daughter was born, they bought their first house; their son was born, and they bought a bigger house. That was just the way it was for them and their friends. No one had much money: they played a lot of cards, they drank whatever was the fad of the season, they joined the church, and vacations were either extended car trips or tent camping. Bev endured the latter exactly once.

Bison usually could not wait to get to work. He liked and admired most of his colleagues and found the work meaningful. He found the politics of the workplace quite challenging: he'd always had a temper and found that it was occasionally useful in helping his coworkers understand their particular shortcomings. This trait was not career-enhancing, but his lab-wide reputation as a problem solver meant he was widely respected if not always liked. And he was compensated only slightly less than what he felt he deserved.

He was most content at home with his family. Just like his parents had been, he was happily involved in his community. He was the instigator and peacekeeper for the neighborhood ball games in the front yard, and he and Bev taught Sunday school classes, led the Boy and Girl Scout troops, headed up the PTA, and even taught a course to teenagers on human sexuality.

Inevitably the kids grew up, wrecked a few cars, made it safely to and from a few proms, and went off to college. Bev ran a consulting business, and at the end of a busy day they would share stories of human foibles over dinner.

In the late 1970s, the middle-aged, somewhat rotund Bison became deeply immersed in a multiple-national study to devise a proliferation-proof nuclear fuel cycle.

He deeply admired his boss on the project, Milt, because of Milt's ability to manage people. For his part, Milt was always afraid that Bison was going to incur a security infraction because of his desk, a cluttered surface on which classified and unclassified material commingled in a seemingly random fashion.

"Bise," the exasperated Milt cajoled one afternoon as he laid a Snickers bar on Bison's desk, "would you do me a favor and try to clear off that desk? You're about to give me an ulcer."

Irritated at the interruption, Bison tersely answered, "Which would you prefer—neatness or proficiency?"

"Oh, I'd settle for either," was Milt's smiling reply, which was followed briefly by Bison's all-out burst of laughter. "And while you're in one of your rare jovial moods, I do have another favor I'd like to ask of you."

"That sounds serious. Do you have another candy bar?"

"I am serious. I'd like to have you think about taking over the nuclear counterterrorism program for me. Right now, it's just not working. Good people, tremendously interesting problems, plenty of money, but it simply is not working. I think it needs the Bison touch."

"Because you're my friend, I'll think about it. But I can tell you right now that I'd rather not. This proliferation stuff might prove very important. It's intriguing, and I'm happy."

Bison was surprised that it took Milt two entire days to return. "Have you thought any more about that opportunity I offered you the other day?"

"Yes, I did. I'm very flattered by the offer but I think I'd like to stay where I am."

"That's final?" Milt answered, looking disappointed.

"Yeah, I think so."

Two hours later Milt's boss appeared in Bison's doorway. "Hey, Bise, Milt tells me you're not exactly jumping at the opportunity to run the counterterrorism program. I believe that is one of the most important programs in this organization and, quite frankly, I've been rather embarrassed by our lack of progress. Both Milt and I believe that you can straighten it out. I'd certainly appreciate it if you'd reconsider your decision."

Bison might have been a bit slow in understanding nuances of political situations, but he was not completely dense. Reconsidering his decision led him to the Parisian Catacombs that September afternoon in 1995.

CHAPTER TWO
Evgeny

"What did they say? Are they going to let you go?"

"I didn't ask. Something came up. I decided it would be better to talk about it tonight. Tonight for sure." Fifteen-year-old Evgeny's voice was strained, his usual exuberance entirely absent. He was about to test the boundaries of his close-knit, loving family. The implicit assumption had always been that as soon as he finished the ninth form at school, he would go to work to help support his family. But lately he had become aware of other possibilities. He now wanted a brighter future, and he knew that his restless nature would not be satisfied by a life like that of his father, a man who had spent nearly thirty years working in the dirty and dangerous underground mines.

Evgeny's desire to deviate from the expected path was not really surprising. He was extremely slight of build, unlike his brawny, wide-shouldered father. He was content to stay inside, spending long hours reading and sketching Southern Ural scenes while his siblings and other boys from the village were playing boisterously outdoors. While his male friends were beginning to demonstrate lustful ambitions toward their female companions, Evgeny had not yet reached that stage, and his gaze inadvertently shifted to his feet whenever he found himself in a one-on-one discussion with a member of the opposite sex. His good nature ensured that he was well liked, but lately he had been uncharacteristically quiet and withdrawn.

Life around his hometown of Zlatoust in the Southern Urals had always been hard. The collectivization of the post-World War II Soviet regime resulted in grandiose promises but a different reality. The state provided employment, free education, inexpensive housing, and medical care, but the price was enormous. An inept and corrupt administration meant that the collectivization system would never work, leading to low morale, low productivity, high inflation, and the scarcity of almost everything.

Evgeny's family made the best of the situation. His father, Dmitry, traced his ancestry in the local area back five generations and took immense pride in his heritage. He was well respected by all who knew him and dearly loved by his wife and three sons. His work in one of the nearly played-out magnetite mines dotting the southern Urals did not make him rich, but there was always food on his family's table.

The Ovstronov home was full of laughter and love. Dmitry led the family with a stern tongue and a tender heart. More from a sense of civic duty than any religious or political beliefs, he and his wife, Iridia, encouraged their boys in the Russian Orthodox faith and saw that they participated in the Pioneer and Komsomol Soviet youth organizations. "It can't hurt and it might help," the boys were told. "And," repeating the guidance of parents everywhere, "it will build character."

Evgeny and his brothers respected their parents and understood that the elder Ovstronovs had their sons' best interests at heart. So how in the world could Evgeny explain his plan? How could he explain that he wanted more for himself than his father had been granted? That night at dinner his mind raced as he silently practiced his appeal.

He was so caught up in his thoughts that he had not heard his mother. "Evgeny! For the third time, what on earth is bothering you?"

"Um, I have something I need to talk to you and Daddy about...."

Sensing Evgeny's discomfort, Dmitry sent the two younger boys away from the table and asked, "What could be so difficult, son?"

"I don't want to upset you, but when I finish the ninth form I want to go to secondary school. All my teachers—"

"Stop! Stop! Enough! Not a chance," Dmitry exploded, his face turning red. "I can't believe that you'd even have such a notion. Don't you know how hard your mother and I work to keep this family together, how tough it is to occasionally have a bit of meat in addition to our soup? You like pelmeni, don't you? And kvass once in a while? I'm ashamed of you for asking and ashamed of myself for having raised such a selfish son!" Glaring at Evgeny, Dmitry stormed out of the house.

Throughout the next week the family meals were silent, and the generally loquacious Dmitry did little more than grunt. Evgeny spent the week trying to figure out how to get back in his father's good graces while he tried to resign himself to a future in the mines.

One night he sat down to dinner, and Dmitry looked at him with a half smile. "Son, your mother and I have been talking and we believe that, if you'd like to, you should continue with your schooling after the end of this year.

We'd like you and your brothers to have an easier life than we've had and believe secondary school is almost necessary these days. We know you feel that it is your obligation to help us, but we've gotten by this far and"—he finally showed the smile Evgeny so dearly loved—"we can probably survive another two years."

Evgeny had never been happier than he was at vocational-technical school. He focused on machine design, and the field was a perfect fit for his talents and interests. For the first time in his life he felt that he was using his mind to its full potential. When the two-year course was over, he did not dare consider going on to a gymnasium. His family could not afford to spend any more money on his schooling, and he needed to figure out how he was going to fulfill his compulsory military obligation.

Shortly after returning home from school, Evgeny caught up with his boyhood friend Vadim, who had enlisted in the navy the fall after he had finished the ninth form. An unlikely duo, Vadim and Evgeny complemented each other and had been inseparable throughout their early years. Evgeny was studious and serious, always pushing himself, while the fun-loving Vadim always looked for the easy way out of any situation. The friends appreciated the other's differences, and there was no one either trusted more.

Now Vadim was full of stories about his wild experiences in the Soviet navy, with a particular emphasis on his escapades during shore leave. Evgeny had known Vadim long enough to suspect that many of these stories were not exactly true but still found it amusing to sit back and laugh at their telling.

Although Vadim made the navy sound like a great way to fulfill his military commitment, Evgeny decided to enlist in the army because it entailed a two-year stint while the navy demanded three. After three months of basic training and six weeks of technical school, he found himself at a nuclear weapons depot outside Leningrad.

"There is so much to learn," he wrote home. "I'm spending most of my free time in Leningrad. The art here is simply amazing; all of the pictures from the textbooks are hanging right there on the wall."

He neglected to tell his parents that his most significant discovery was not cultural. It was Lilia. A flirtatious, redheaded fusing technician, the young woman had caught the eye of all the single men on the depot and many of the married ones. He did not know it, but Evgeny had become a remarkably handsome young man and looked as if he had been born to wear a uniform. His confidence did not match his looks, though. He had spent almost every spare moment of the past decade with his head in a book and had no idea how to talk to a woman. Every time he crossed paths with Lilia, he found himself blushing and stammering. And he knew she sensed the effect she had on him and, even worse, he could tell that she enjoyed it.

After weeks of agony, Evgeny decided to take the risk. So the first time a chance to talk to Lilia presented itself, he asked if she would like to go into Leningrad with him.

"I don't know," she said with a smile. "But my plans for tomorrow just fell through because Arseny can't get away. I guess I can go with you, but you weren't planning on staying the night, were you?"

"Well, ahh, no, I wasn't," Evgeny stammered, uncertain what on earth he had gotten himself into, and somewhat shocked by Lilia's forwardness. Spend the night! Good lord, he'd barely had the courage to ask her out!

Four months later it was Evgeny's parents' turn to be shocked. "Dear Mom and Dad," the letter home read, "I'm getting married. Lilia is pregnant. Please be excited for me, because this is absolutely wonderful news. I can't wait until you meet her; you'll adore her as much as I do."

Evgeny's letters to his mom and dad had been full of Lilia—"she's beautiful, we like all the same things, we think alike, she makes me laugh, I've never felt this way"—but they had not met her. And, when they got this latest letter, they were pretty sure they did not like her. They did not travel to Leningrad for the wedding.

The couple was wed with the irascible Vadim somehow managing to wrangle leave from the navy so that he could stand by Evgeny's side. Dmitry and Iridia did not meet their new daughter-in-law for another year, until Evgeny was discharged. With Lilia and six-month-old Eugenia in tow, he returned to the Chelyabinsk Oblast.

When Iridia answered the door, she wasn't certain it was her firstborn standing in front of her. The eyes seemed right and there was that old impish grin, but could this actually be her Evgeny? This person was about half a foot taller than Dmitry. The smallish, timid boy who had left them two years ago had appeared to be a mishmash of disparate parts; the man who now stood before her was so well put together. The shoulders were broad, the stomach flat, and the military-requisite moustache well trimmed and dark. A slim, exceedingly attractive, apprehensive young woman stood at his side; a petite little girl, dressed in her Sunday best, fidgeted about their legs. All doubt of who this attractive group was disappeared with the man's "Hi, Mom" as he reached out to embrace her.

The afternoon was long. Pleasantries were exchanged but it was a brittle, difficult conversation with both couples exceedingly ill-at-ease. Then Eugenia crawled onto Iridia's lap. The little girl's charm captivated both Dmitry and Iridia and, later that evening, in private, the elder Ostronovs agreed that perhaps Lilia wasn't so bad. And wasn't Eugenia the cutest little girl they had ever seen?

The young family found a small one-room home between Zlatoust and

Miass, and Evgeny started his work assignment at a state-run farm machinery production facility, a more financially advantageous position than working at one of the collectives because he received actual wages and benefits rather than only his share of the collective's profits.

"Guess what I heard last night?" the ever-present Vadim, recently returned from the navy and now working on a tractor assembly line, greeted him with one evening. "I hear that they're looking for a few experienced technicians up at Zlatoust-36. Think we should apply?"

"Are you out of your mind?" was Evgeny's immediate, emotional response. He was totally amazed that his friend would even consider such a thing.

• • •

The Zlatoust-36 plant was located in the town of Tryokhgorny, some seventy kilometers southwest of Zlatoust. It was one of southern Ural's "white cities," the key locations of the Soviet's nuclear weapon complex. So secret that they did not even appear on maps, these cities and the byproducts of their industry were reviled by the citizens of the surrounding Oblast countryside.

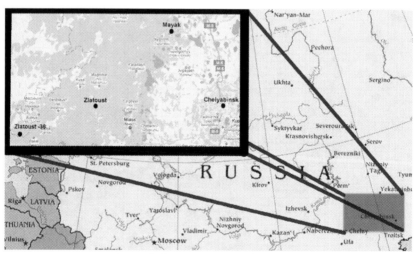

Map of Zlatoust Area, Southern Urals

For centuries the area, intensely rich in natural minerals and abundant farmland, had been the nation's center of iron production; in the early twentieth century, metallurgical industries based upon steel fabrication abounded. Tractor factories—and during the war, tank production—employed almost 10 percent of the local workforce. The area also supplied such diverse products as construction materials, clothing, and meat and dairy products.

After World War II, under the Soviet collectivization regimes, these independent enterprises slowly died and a new industry took its place. Because of its sparse population and relative isolation, the southern Urals were chosen as the home of much of the Soviet Union's nuclear weapon program, a program conducted with virtually no regard for the safety of the people who lived in the area or for the preservation of their environment. Everything was enacted with absolute secrecy and imposing physical security. The populace was, however, aware that an entire underground city had been built in the mid 1940s on the bank of Lake Kyzyltash. It was, with some substantiating evidence, widely believed that some seventy thousand inmates from Soviet labor camps had been conscripted to build this Mayak complex and that practically all of these prisoners had died within five years. What the inhabitants of the area did know for sure was that an abnormally high incidence of cancer suddenly occurred in the villages which lined the Techna River, downstream from Mayak; the Techna was the source of these villages' drinking water. When asked, the Soviet officials feigned ignorance and claimed that the increase in cancer fatalities was not statistically significant.

In 1957 there was an explosion in one of the "forbidden" areas surrounding Mayak. The subsequent ground shock was felt as far away as twenty kilometers and was followed by a strange, hovering black cloud that caused the authorities to immediately evacuate several villages. The reason for all of this, according to the patently untrue cover story circulated by the Soviets, was a massive crude oil accident. According to the cover-up, the oil had spread into the region's fields and groundwater. Selected people, based on ethnic background and including schoolchildren as young as ten years old, were forced to participate in an enormous cleanup effort, burying cattle killed as a result of the "oil spill," scrubbing contaminated bricks, and digging up potatoes and carrots with their bare hands and disposing of them in giant pits. When members of the cleanup crews developed afflictions and illnesses they could not even pronounce, Soviet authorities continued to deny that a radiation accident was responsible. Cancer was never listed as the cause of death on any official documents; the authorities worried that doing so would reveal the location of the nuclear weapon production facilities.

Then, during the drought of 1967, all the lakes and rivers in the area dried up. This included Lake Karachay, which the Soviets had used as a dumping basin for radioactive waste. Gale-force winds spread the radioactive dust from the dry lakebed over twenty-five thousand square kilometers. Residents with crude radiation measuring devices calculated a radioactive release of about five million curies, approximately the same as that at Hiroshima. The authorities continued to insist that there had been no radioactivity in the area and that the horrifying illnesses many of the inhabitants suffered were coincidental and not the result of radiation.

Some residents demanded to be resettled by the authorities, and some moved away on their own. Most, however, stayed—because their roots were there, because they did not have sufficient resources to move, because they feared an inability to find a job elsewhere, or simply because they knew no other life. But the fact that they stayed did not mean that their anger had subsided or that they looked any more kindly upon their fellow residents who chose to work at Zlatoust-36.

On one hand, it was easy to understand why someone would want to work in one of the closed cities. Only the original Mayak facility was underground, and the rest of the closed cities looked, on the surface, like any other community in the southern Urals, albeit with guards. Working at these facilities brought unimagined prosperity and unparalleled living conditions. The complexes paid salaries that substantially exceeded the state-wage rates and the stores were stocked with "unobtainable" foods, liquor, excellent clothing, and jewelry at extremely low prices.

On the other hand, though, residents of these communities paid an enormous cost in terms of personal freedom. The nuclear workers looked carefree and wealthy to outsiders, but their lives were highly controlled, with every action subjected to official scrutiny and intimidation. Traffic in and out of the cities was tightly controlled. There was no pretense of democracy or anything resembling civic life. Service to the facility was paramount: a worker's social standing was a direct reflection upon his or her role in the laboratory, and a rancorous discussion with a boss in the afternoon could result in the employee and his family having vanished by the following morning.

All this history was at play when Vadim suggested that they look for work at "Thirty-Six."

"Vadim, you know I can't. The nuclear programs have destroyed our land and probably are right now destroying us. We don't know how much radiation we've received or if it's even safe to live here, and they won't tell us. How could I ever work for someone I don't trust and who has done this to our homeland, to our people?"

"C'mon, Evgeny, you're way too idealistic. That's all history. Be realistic. Think about the money and the benefits. Those guys up there aren't any smarter than we are, don't work any harder than we do, and they get paid so much more than we do. Why not us? Think about Eugenia."

"I am thinking about Eugenia. All I do is think about Lilia and Eugenia and how my parents love them. I can't risk alienating my parents again by going up there. It's different for you, but my family means everything to me, and you know how my dad feels about the evils of the Ministry of Atomic Energy. Of course I want more money. But that cost, it's just too much."

Lilia did not share any of Evgeny's reservations when he told her about

Vadim's suggestion. She giggled and came running over to give him a hug, her long red hair flowing behind her. She was more animated than Evgeny had seen her in months. "So what if the state tries to run our lives, how could it be much worse than it is now? Just look at how we could live. We'd have a real home for our family and finally have some money. And," she added with her mischievous smile, "I could buy some slinky lingerie."

"Stop teasing," Evgeny scolded, although the vision of the lingerie made him smile. "This is serious. The idea sickens me. Even if I wanted to do it, teaming with Vadim would be worrisome. You know how close we've always been. I really enjoy his company, but if we apply together, they might consider me one of a pair of loose cannons."

"Well, you know how I feel about him," Lilia answered. "I think he's slightly insane. I've always thought he was a bad influence on you, and I've seen that wistful look you get when he describes his latest escapade. I honestly fear that some day he's going to lead you astray."

"Oh stop, you know I'm stronger than that. But do you think that I should take the chance to discuss the possibility of going out there with Mom and Dad?"

"Absolutely. I don't think that it's so unreasonable and I think your mom, at least, will agree with me."

"Perhaps you're right. But I sure don't look forward to talking to Dad. He's going to be livid."

And he was.

"You can't be serious!" Dmitry roared. "You know how people in the valley feel about working up there! You'll be a traitor; you'll have joined the enemy. We won't get to see Eugenia. That will break your mom's heart. Don't you care about that?"

When Dmitry paused to catch a breath, Iridia broke in. "I do love that girl so much and it kills me to see what those people have done to our valley. But what's done is done, and we can't do anything about that now. And, Dmitry, I think we need to be practical. What kind of future do Evgeny and Lilia really have now? I hate where they live and so do you, and I don't know how they'll ever be able to move anywhere else. This might sound terrible to us now but perhaps we should at least consider it. And how many young people in the valley these days would even consult their parents before making such a decision?"

Dmitry lifted Eugenia up into this lap. "You know how much I despise these arrogant outsiders who've come in and desecrated our beautiful valley," Dmitry continued, although his tone had softened considerably. "But I can understand why you would want to go there; there certainly are advantages. But you don't know how I hate the thought of not getting to see this one as often"—kissing the top of Eugenia's head—"and you and Lilia, of course," smiling as it became apparent that his daughter-in-law and son were afterthoughts. "If it's as good there as people say, it would be a real opportunity. But if it's not, you'll have to live with that decision and you certainly will have alienated a lot of friends here in the valley. But it's got to be your decision, not ours."

Iridia gave her husband a long look, a look encompassing years of marriage and mutual respect. "Dmitry, if you were Evgeny, would you go? Tell me the truth."

Dmitry grunted, lit his pipe, and stared at his family for several minutes. During the long silence, Lilia reached over and grabbed Evgeny's hand.

Finally he spoke. "Yes, I expect that I would. I don't have to like it, but it is a chance for a better future. I would sure hate to see Evgeny spending thirty years in that mine."

Within a month, Vadim and Evgeny were in a government taxi driving through the secret city on the way to their interviews. "Let them interview us separately, let them interview us separately," was Evgeny's silent supplication.

Fortunately, the three-hour interview/interrogations were separate. The exhaustive process covered their capabilities and experiences and, not particularly guardedly, probed into their political philosophies. *If we'd interviewed together, and if Vadim had shared some of his provocative anticommunist beliefs with the officials,* Evgeny thought, *we would probably both already be on our way out.*

More relaxed during the taxi ride after the interviews, they looked out the windows at the passing city. Carefree kids on their way home from school teased and jostled one another on well-trimmed lawns in front of newly painted duplex and triplex housing. Street sweepers were busy at work, and mail carriers walked their routes.

True to form, Vadim again pushed the limit. "Gosh, it would be great to drive around and see the city before we leave," he suggested to the driver. His suggestion was ignored and the driver took the same direct route back to the city exit they had followed earlier in the day.

Neither Evgeny nor Vadim heard anything from Zlatoust-36 for three months. It was an anxious wait: not only were they concerned about their applications, but several mutual friends, alerted to their applications by authorities conducting background checks, treated them with a new coolness. Although, Vadim reported gleefully, several of his female friends had suddenly become much more interested in him; this interest, he admitted, might have more to do with the possibility of living a luxurious life in Zlatoust-36 that it did with his many charms.

One Saturday morning a van pulled up to Evgeny's home. Evgeny was again escorted into the closed city, given a four-hour-long "grilling," offered a technician's job at more than double his current income, shown the floor plan for a two-bedroom villa, and told that he had until 8:00 am the next morning to make a decision about his future.

By the next morning, Evgeny and Lilia had not only reached a decision, they had moved. They all, Evgeny, Lilia, Eugenia and two-month-old Cassandra, spent Sunday evening exclaiming over the air conditioning and rubbing their bare feet through the wall-to-wall carpet in their new home. Eugenia was so excited by the luxury that Lilia let her put some blankets and pillows down and sleep that night on their "cushy" floor.

Vadim never heard a thing about his application and was afraid to pursue the matter. With his limited financial prospects, he undertook the initial steps to join the Communist Party of the Soviet Union. He was on the path to becoming a functionary, an apparatchik—the very sort of person he had always ridiculed and claimed to despise.

Evgeny, Eugenia, Cassandra, and Lilia spent the first few months at 36 adjusting to life behind the fence. They were literally shut off from the world; little information flowed into or out of the city, although they were allowed infrequent visits to see Dmitry and Iridia. Behavior was governed by community standards and expectations, as well as by a healthy fear of the authorities. They observed firsthand the disappearance of people who chose to challenge the standards or authorities.

But Evgeny and Lilia went along with the system, and the family prospered. The schools were good, there was meat on the table, and their social life was enjoyable.

Evgeny's career proceeded smoothly. His job was challenging, but his restless nature had him convinced that he could manage the entire complex much more efficiently and productively than it was currently being operated. But of course this could never happen since he had neither a gymnasium degree nor high-up political connections. He could live with this, though, because Lilia and the girls were so carefree and happy. And there was a brand new Lada 1600 in their driveway and a whole drawer full of sexy lingerie.

Then came December 1991. After years of progressive dissolution, the Soviet Union collapsed. Early the next month, the Ministry for Atomic Energy authorities appeared in Zlatoust-36. "Pack up all your personal belongings and be gone from the plant by 5:00 pm" the facility's public address system blared.

It was all over. The entire social structure of Zlatoust-36's once proud, cloistered, select society had irreversibly changed, and all its highly specialized workers were now unemployed. "You will be notified by the end of the week when to pick up your back wages. You have thirty days to vacate the city," the PA continued.

The Faustian agreement inflicted upon the people of the Chelyabinsk was over. For decades, the area's residents had unwillingly traded the environmental health of their homeland for the prosperity of a select few. In the end, everyone lost. The region was severely contaminated by radiation and the high-paying jobs had disappeared overnight. The government had neither the interest nor the desire to clean up the mess they had created, and the post-Soviet economy held out little hope for employment. Gorbachev's perestroika reforms of the late 1980s had attempted to convert the state-run economy to one governed by market forces, but ultimately the dismantling of the planned economy resulted in complete chaos with shortages of goods in grocery stores, massive budget deficits, and out-of-control inflation. Jobs were no longer guaranteed and several million people throughout the former Soviet Union were unemployed. And with the shuttering of Zlatoust-36 and its sister plants, some fifty thousand skilled technicians were suddenly cast adrift on a faltering local economy.

Through some friends of his parents, Evgeny and Lilia found an affordable three-room house near his parents. But no one seemed to be able to help with the employment situation.

"I don't know what to do," Evgeny confided to Lilia after a month of fruitless job hunting. "There are no jobs. I've tried everything." Tight-lipped and furious, Lilia fought to keep her temper. She could not even look at Evgeny, because if she did she knew it would only lead to another of the couple's almost daily arguments. Evgeny, she was convinced, needed to forget his expectations about a salary to match what he earned at 36; he could not seem to accept that it just wasn't going to happen. And while he was at it, she fumed to herself, he should throw away the idea that the job he found needed to be enjoyable. The family needed food on the table; at this point she felt enjoying the job should not be a high priority.

The family, settling into another evening of silent reproach and worry, were pleasantly surprised by the unexpected knock on the door. There stood a bearded, beaming Vadim, as expansive as ever.

"Come in, come in," Lilia cried, happy to see the man she had once considered a bad influence on her husband. "We haven't seen you forever. Let's have a drink and catch up. Evgeny, find the kvass we brought from 36. Vadim, tell us everything...."

Over another bottle and a half of kvass Vadim settled into his natural role of storyteller. It turned out that he had risen into the management bureaucracy at the tractor factory. Evgeny suspected that Vadim's success was a result of his Soviet Party affiliation, but he realized that he was hardly in the position to criticize anyone's employment status.

"It's really not such a bad place," Vadim went on. "I don't know what you're doing now, but if you're interested, I think I could probably arrange a job for you, Evgeny. Just think, we'd be together again."

"Oh, Vadim, could you?" Lilia asked before Evgeny had a chance to speak, quickly forgetting her previous reservations about the man's character.

"I think I could. And I might be able to finagle a better starting salary than most people get. After all, I do have quite a bit of pull there."

"What is the starting salary?" Evgeny reluctantly asked. He knew that with Lilia this animated, he had better at least consider the job, even though it was not at all what he envisioned for his future.

When Vadim mentioned the figure, Evgeny blanched. "But that's a third of what I was making! We could never live on that!"

"What about me?" Lilia asked, afraid an opportunity was about to be lost. "Aren't there a lot of women working on the assembly line? We could both work there."

"You could," Vadim agreed, "but that assembly line is boring and monotonous work. Would you really be interested?"

Evgeny started to protest Lilia's scheme but then realized that it might be their only realistic option. He remembered from their days in the military that Lilia had really enjoyed working, especially around men. But maybe, just maybe, this was the family's solution, at least temporarily.

"I know your mom would love to watch the girls," Lilia said, turning to Evgeny with the first spark of enthusiasm he'd seen in weeks. "She told me just the other day that she was tired of being by herself all day now that your brothers are gone and your dad's away at work."

Vadim, Evgeny, and Lilia toasted the younger Ovstronov family's future with another bottle of kvass.

• • •

Evgeny's and Lilia's new dawn-to-dusk schedule did not leave a lot of time for the family life they had once cherished, but Lilia enjoyed both her job and the time she and Evgeny shared driving to and from work together. She enjoyed the often off-color banter with her mostly male colleagues on the assembly line, and she was particularly happy knowing that she was contributing to the family. She tried to keep her enthusiasm hidden from her husband, because she knew that he felt her need to work was a reflection on what he felt was his masculine duty to provide for his family.

Plus, Evgeny wasn't enjoying his job. Some days he would hardly say anything on the way home from work, and other days the ride was filled with lamentations of management's poor decisions. Over and over he would complain that merit had little to do with career advancement, and that he could see no chance of his advancing in pay grade, with an even lesser possibility of moving to a position where he could use his design skills. Lilia expected, but never suggested to Evgeny, that a large part of his unhappiness was that the much-less qualified Vadim had a job that was several pay grades above his own. When he and Lilia had time together in the evening, he often would withdraw from the family conversation and just sit in his chair sketching farm equipment designs. Lilia knew that he longed to build prototypes of his designs but did not have the money to do that, and that made matters that much worse. Individual entrepreneurship was encouraged in the new Russia, but where could a factory worker get the necessary financing to become an entrepreneur?

CHAPTER THREE
Masud

Missing Person—Masud Sawalha, Sunni, Economist. Born 1954 to Prof. and Mrs. Garai Sawalha of Cairo. Educated at Azhar Institute and Al-Azhar University, PhD 1978. Employed by Ministry of Trade and Industry. Last seen at Al-Azhar in May 1986. Classified listing, Cairo Daily News, June 11, 1988.

Masud never saw the classified listing, but if he had he would have been both saddened and amused. He knew he wasn't missing; he knew exactly where he was. And he knew that he was absolutely drained from his six-mile training run in the desert of Northwestern Sudan. The run, along with target practice and field instruction on stalking, killing, and escape from captivity were all part of his daily routine. Masud Sawalha was not a missing economist. Masud Sawalha was a member of Takfir wa Hijra, one of the world's most radical international terrorist networks. Becoming a terrorist had been a saddening, heartbreaking decision—one he could not have imagined when he graduated from Al-Azhar.

There was a lot he could not have imagined during those years at Al-Azhar. Only a few years had passed, but to Masud it was a lifetime ago that he and his friends gathered in the courtyard of the university's mosque, debating the important events of the days.

On one such afternoon Masud held forth, as he frequently did. "How can we believe any of it? They all make promises—Nasser, Sadat, Mubarak, all of them—promises of great change but nothing happens. Our parents continually tell us that if we just wait patiently everything will improve; our living conditions will become tolerable, we will regain the respect we deserve—Inshallah, God willing, they say. So we wait. And still nothing changes. It can't be Allah's will that we just wait.

"How can we continue to ignore—it seems we even condone—the Israeli expansionism and the insensitivity and arrogance that we continually receive from the Europeans and the Americans? I'm tired of being subjected to that smugness, that air of superiority, that condescension. Has everybody forgotten that at one time—while Europe was still floundering in the Dark Ages and there wasn't even an America—that we had the world's highest standard of living, the most efficient and humane government, and that we led the world in literature, science, medicine, and philosophy?"

Year after year, Masud simmered, fighting to retain his patience. By 1986 he was no longer sure what he was expecting to change. He was a thirty-two-year-old economist with a PhD from Al-Azhar University, the Islamic world's most prestigious university. Yet he was employed as a mid-level bureaucrat working for the Egyptian government and making one hundred and forty Egyptian pounds, or about forty American dollars, per month. His future was not bright and his ambition was not fulfilled. He sensed that this dissatisfaction was carrying over into his personal life. He remembered once feeling lighthearted, but now everything seemed so serious and hopeless.

Masud had enjoyed a wonderful childhood in Cairo. His middle-class parents were cosmopolitan and educated, and they coddled their handsome, studious son. They raised him to believe that he could do anything he wanted to do, and that the world was a pleasant place waiting to bestow its delights upon the charming Masud.

By the 1980s Cairo had lost many of its pleasures. Masud still appreciated living in the intellectual, religious, and educational center of the Arabian world. But the city was rapidly deteriorating; no municipality could withstand the influx of nearly a million illiterate persons per year and survive when there was no money or assistance devoted to accommodating these new arrivals. Travel through the city by vehicle of any kind had become almost impossible because of the absence of traffic control and the ensuing gridlock. Travel by foot was equally undesirable because of the increasing squalor and filth; the sixty thousand zabbaleen, the freelance garbage collectors, could no longer keep up with the amount of waste that was being generated. The Egyptian leadership seemed to be completely incapable of correcting any of these social and economic injustices. There was always another array of promising new programs; each of these seemed to end up profiting the upper class of the society and leaving the lower classes in a continual struggle between hopelessness and desperation.

Masud was not pleased with himself either. He began to realize that, despite all his degrees, he was undereducated. He had never been taught to think, to solve problems. The national education system, with its almost exclusive focus on religion, was not properly preparing students for life in the modern world. Sure, he had followed the traditional path: he had memorized the Koran, and he had attended the most prestigious university in the nation. In retrospect, he realized that most everything he had learned of practical value was acquired from the informal discussions with the mullahs in the courtyards of Al-Azhar.

His job at the Ministry of Trade and Industry was a joke. In the 1960s Nasser had insisted that each of the forty thousand yearly college graduates be guaranteed a government job. This attempt at civil service modernization had led to a government bureaucracy of more than two million people, a system so clogged by local fiefdoms that it was impossible to produce positive results. There were presently five times as many people as were needed in Masud's department. He had a shared desk with no telephone and no work. Egyptian bureaucracy, he was totally convinced, lived up to its reputation of being "the curse of the Pharaohs."

And the future? Masud's monthly salary was less than that of an illiterate maid in the homes of the elite in Egyptian society; in ten years he could aspire to a senior diplomat position with a monthly salary of only five hundred Egyptian pounds per month. Making matters even worse, he was going to be called up for his compulsory military duty at any time. Duty in the Egyptian army was anything but arduous, but the pay of five dollars per month meant that practically all draftees were forced to find moonlighting jobs. That was a proposition that looked even worse than his Ministry job.

Every afternoon, after a few unproductive hours at the office, Masud and his colleagues would congregate and bemoan their dismal futures, joining their favorite mullahs at either Al-Azhar or one of the neighborhood mosques. They would discuss the options for forcing societal change. They found that most of the mullahs not only shared their disenchantment, many even advocated violence as necessary to accomplish reform. Some, particularly those at Al-Azhar, were quite adept at interpreting the Koran to justify this violence or almost any other action that they, the mullahs, might advocate.

By temperament a pacifist, Masud was surprised to find himself gradually agreeing with those who believed that terrorism was the only solution to the dilemma. He lay awake nights wondering if this could possibly be true. Could violence somehow generate the impetus for constructive change?

Lengthy conservations with his parents, whom he loved and respected, yielded few rewards. He sought guidance, but the nightly explorations of political philosophy and possible ways to improve Cairenes' existence would invariably end up in disagreement and, as was more recently the case, shouting matches.

He hated the shouting and knew that his strong relationship with his father was in trouble. He could no longer tolerate his father's recommendation to trust in Allah. It wasn't only his father; all of his immediate family became involved in these discussions, and often the extended family was summoned to talk sense into Masud. Invariably, when everyone had restated their position and all tempers had subsided, the unanimous advice to the distraught Masud was Inshallah.

Masud's eventual acceptance of violent action as the answer to his desperation and hopelessness was strongly influenced by the enigmatic Manu. No one was really sure when Manu had joined their informal discussion group, and no one remembered actually being introduced to him. He just seemed to have materialized from the throng of young scholars that congregated around the university. Before long, he was a regular participant in the group's discussions, eventually coming to share its intellectual leadership with Masud.

Manu was about the same age as the rest of the group, also a PhD, and also a civil servant, working in the Ministry of Foreign Exchange. He strongly but quietly advocated not only taking decisive actions against America and Europeans but also against the Egyptian government itself because it had accepted rule by people he considered non-Muslim. The young men in the mosque courtyard thought his eloquence and persuasiveness were almost Mohammedan.

Over the course of several months, Masud grew close to Manu, close enough to socialize. Masud was pleased to accept Manu's invitation to a meeting of an anti-government "logistics" organization. After attending several of these meetings, which Masud found quite enjoyable, with lots of laughter, he realized that the group was interested in more than just logistics and that Manu was more than just another discontented civil servant. He was, Masud finally recognized, a recruiter for the terrorist organization Takfir wa Hijra, an organization following in the footsteps of the martyred Sayyid Qutb.

Realizing that he was being recruited, Masud was torn. Was he ready for an irreversible break with his family? Were such drastic measures really the way to right Egypt's ills? Was it some kind of omen that his army induction notice arrived during this period of personal agonizing?

One of the things that helped Masud appease his sense of guilt over abandoning his old world was that members of Takfir were not bound by the usual Islamic constraints. They adopted non-Islamic appearances, shaved their beards, and wore Western apparel in order to blend inconspicuously into their community. They were permitted to drink alcohol, eat pork, and dance— anything they felt would help them achieve their objectives. Most amazing to

Masud was that they actually recruited females into the group. While this was contrary to all of his ingrained beliefs about the role of women in society, he could see its usefulness if they were to pass themselves as Westerners.

The organization was comprised of a series of small cells located around the globe, including a few in the United States where their members enjoyed being church deacons and PTA presidents while secretly carrying out objectives of the Takfir organization. Their goal was always foremost in their minds: to do whatever was required to revolutionize the Egyptian government and destroy the heathen Western society.

Masud found the option of living like a Westerner quite appealing, and he knew his light complexion would help him pass as a European. But he was still extremely uncomfortable with the thought that his assignment could well entail indiscriminate killing. It angered and sickened him that the possibility of injuring large numbers of people who were just in the wrong place at the wrong time seemed to excite so many of his fellow initiates. While many of the possible Takfir operations that Masud and his fellow recruiters rather superficially discussed seemed reasonable and doable, he felt that some of the "spectaculars," which got everyone highly excited, like attacks on US cities and bombing of Al-Azhar University, were neither practical nor beneficial.

Masud and five other inductees were initiated one evening in a small room lit only with candlelight and clouded with dense incense smoke. The ceremony was conducted by a pair of sheiks who would alternately recite verses of the Koran, interspersed with, "Are you ready for martyrdom?" asked over and over to each of the inductees. On and on this ritual continued, finally terminating with each recruit taking an oath on the Koran and exiting the ceremony with a stated willingness to eliminate as many infidels as necessary to meet the group's objectives.

Masud's eventual decision, which he had convinced himself was inescapable, was devastating to him. He bundled up his beloved dog and went to his parents' house when he knew they weren't home. The note was simple: "Please take care of Akil for me. I'll always love you."

It was the toughest thing he had ever done in his life. Although he never saw the missing person notice in the Daily Star, this hurt would have been intensified by being reminded that his nurturing family continued to love and worry about him.

• • •

The Takfir training in the Darfur region of northwest Sudan was far more intense than even the athletic Masud had expected: running, weight training, obstacle courses, forced marches, weapon firing and cleaning, weeks alone in the desert learning to survive and trying to find his way back to base, more running, different weapons, and on and on. After four months, he was exhausted but had could now run fifteen hundred kilometers in less than five minutes.

Then, with no break in the physical training came the intensive education into blending with other cultures. Without being told, he knew he had been chosen for some special assignment; his classroom situations and his prescribed classes in the Russian language were strong indicators of his destination. Every day he made mistakes in the situational exercises—mistakes that could have compromised his identity and possibly cost him his life had they occurred in real life. Every day he resolved to concentrate even harder.

Some six months later, he was called before the group leader and given a map that indicated that his assignment was in Zlatoust in the Chelyabinsk Oblast in Southwestern Siberian Russia. His mission was to acquire a nuclear weapon or weapons-grade nuclear material. He was handed a sizeable amount of money and a local contact for any additional needs that might arise. He was told that he would have to find work in Russia to support himself.

His papers and credentials identified him as Aleksy Sidorov, possessor of a Doktor Nauk degree from Sholokov Moscow State University of Humanities. Much to his surprise and annoyance, he was informed that he would not be traveling alone. His classmate Minifu Rahotep, now known as Olga Sidorov, his wife, would accompany him.

Minifu was not Masud's first choice for a wife, even a proxy wife. In fact, of the three women in his recruit class, she would not even have been his second or third choice. It was not that she was unattractive; in fact, she was beautiful. She was short and slender, beautifully proportioned, with curly hair, sparkling blue eyes, and glowing light skin. She constantly exuded sexuality—even after a six-mile run.

She was smart. She proclaimed, and Masud suspected she might be right, that she was the smartest one in the class. But her attitude was unbearable. She trusted no one and was so highly competitive that every simple conversation turned into a verbal contest, a contest she always won because she exhausted her opponent. And this woman, this politically zealous, unlikable woman, was going to act as his wife!

"Look, this masquerade is going to be tough enough without burdening me with someone like Minifu," Masud pleaded with group leader Mose. "It would be so much easier with Bahiti or Khepri, someone I could actually enjoy being around. I would be much more comfortable and certainly less anguished with either of them."

"It wasn't my decision," Mose replied. "I don't know why Minifu was chosen but there's nothing to be done about it. Your only choice is to accept it. And, just so you know, Minifu was here with the same request thirty minutes ago. In addition, she demanded that her new name be Lubov rather than Olga. I said okay, because it was easier than arguing with her. Congratulations, you two are now the happily married Aleksy and Lubov Sidorov."

Knowing when he was beaten, Masud walked away shaking his head, wondering how he was going to face the next several years in a strange environment with a reprehensible "bride."

Aleksy and Lubov packed their few belongings and flew to Moscow where they were met by a Takfir sleeper agent, a clunky and unreliable-looking 1990 Lada sedan, spotless credentials, additional funds, and the name of their "resident keeper," a gentleman in Miass.

The couple was enjoying a tentative civility, each recognizing their mission would be impossible if they were constantly bickering. Somewhere around Ufa, shortly after Lubov insisted on equal driving time, they began to appreciate the diversity of the landscape, leaving the steppe zones of Ufa and entering the forested and mountainous regions in the vicinity of Zlatoust.

Aleksy was happy to let Lubov drive. He was tired, and being a passenger gave him the freedom to consider why the top two buttons of Lubov's blouse were unbuttoned. What was going on? Was some sort of thaw in process? He glanced at her out of the corner of his eye, but she kept her eyes focused on the torn-up road ahead.

As they drove, the couple chatted companionably about what lay ahead, discussing their housing options and the division of household chores.

"It goes without saying," Lubov said anyway, "that we won't share a bedroom."

"Right," Aleksy agreed. "Absolutely right."

Crossing yet another mountain range, the Zlatoust valley and the river Urenga suddenly appeared before them. The view was spectacular; in the distance they could see where the river joined the much larger Ay. The town of Zlatoust was scenically spread along the slopes of the river, going down into the valley and climbing up the steep sides. The excited Aleksy was immediately struck at the contrast of their new home to Cairo. Apparently unimpressed, Lubov demanded that they find someplace to eat.

After a night at what appeared to be the best hotel in town, the couple set out the next morning to scout out jobs and housing. Zlatoust was an industrial town but, to Cairo-bred Aleksy, it seemed spacious and clean. Every tree-lined street led to another park rife with monuments, and even the simplest home had a cheerful, brightly painted front door.

And there seemed to be unlimited employment options: museums, theatres, sports stadiums, and a wide variety of industrial facilities. "I think we'll like this place," Aleksy said, amused that he had caught Lubov smiling. "This might just work out."

By that evening the couple had leased a poorly furnished, third-floor, two-bedroom apartment overlooking the river. Finding employment proved to be much more challenging than they had expected; the area was still in the throes of the ever-diminishing Russian economy and unemployment was still at an all-time high. By the end of the week, Dr. Aleksy had, however, managed to secure an appointment to the gymnasium teaching economics. When he picked up his curriculum materials he realized he was in trouble. He was going to have to learn much more about the analytical methods and logic processes of economics than he had previously been taught. Unexpectedly, he found himself looking forward to the challenge.

Lubov was not as lucky or as happy. The Russian economy was so dire that most women were forced to work to help support their families. This meant that there were more applicants than openings and it was difficult for any woman to find a meaningful job. Lubov finally found a position as an administrative assistant at the Arms Factory, a world-renowned metal engraving company. Her salary was less than one-half Aleksy's rather miserable teacher's stipend. Characteristically, the spirited Lubov was unhappy with this difference, and she managed to mention her dissatisfaction to Aleksy almost daily.

The two salaries enabled them to exist at about the same level as most locals but with very little excess. The enormity of the task that they had been assigned was becoming clearer: very little money, no social contacts, physical appearances that were suspiciously different from most of the locals, and a need to be continually on guard so that their mannerisms did not compromise their assumed identities.

It was proving difficult to develop a social life. People were pleasant, but no one went out of their way to befriend the new couple. Aleksy and Lubov concluded that it was essential to find a way to casually meet and gain the trust of one of the former employees of the near-by Zlatoust-36. Then, through casual conversation, perhaps they could get the information they sought.

They became regulars at the Pomidor, one of the more attractive local cafes. One evening, as they sat at their accustomed table near the door, carefully sipping vodka, a local man, a popular and frequent customer they recognized but had never met, called over to them. "What are you—Americans? Are you going to drink that vodka or are you waiting for it to age?"

The other regulars found this hilarious. Abashed that they had unknowingly exposed themselves, Aleksy and Lubov smiled, finished their drinks, and as quickly as they thought it inconspicuous, waved, and left the Pomidor.

The next evening they went to another cafe and surreptitiously watched the locals drink. Instead of sipping the vodka as they had been doing, they observed that the natives leaned their heads back, tossed the drinks down in one gulp, and chased it with fatty salt herring or a pickled mushroom. Another observation which they made after watching this process for several hours was that it was absolutely socially impermissible to demonstrate any indications of physical impairment induced by vodka consumption.

They practiced drinking like Russians over the next several nights. At home, away from prying eyes, they tossed down one vodka shot after another. "It's so terrible! Why do they do this? Why do we have to do this?" Lubov complained.

"I don't like it either. But we're going to have to do it properly if we're going to be accepted at the Pomidor. Do you have a better idea of how to make friends?"

"Of course I don't. But this is awful!"

On the third night of practice, they began to giggle after the second shot of vodka and pickled mushrooms. Several shots later, neither could remember just why they had found the other so annoying, and after another round, Mr. and Mrs. Aleksy Sidorov became man and wife in more than name. The very next morning, they converted the front bedroom into an office.

"Hey, where have you Americans been? We've missed you!" the guy with the mischievous grin kidded them as he passed their table at the Pomidor a few evenings later. "Come join me and my friends."

As Aleksy and Lubov moved to his table, he continued. "I'm Vadim, and this is my merry band, Gregor, Ivanka, and Ivan." Smiles all around, and after several rounds of vodka, Aleksy and Lubov were no longer outsiders.

The Sidorovs quickly became part of Vadim's regular circle at the Pomidor. All roughly the same age, the group was composed of ten or twelve people on any given night, and they spent hours discussing their jobs, families, love lives, and, their favorite topic, the ridiculousness of the Russian government.

Vadim was the center of every discussion. At the start of an evening he was lighthearted and jovial, but after several vodkas he always returned to his favorite subject, Zlatoust-36 and its part in the destruction of his beloved valley. At least that was his pretension—those who knew him best suspected that his real anger was directed toward the directors of the plant who had failed to hire him, thus excluding him from "the good life."

When Vadim's friends Evgeny and Lilia, who had been residents of Zlatoust-36, occasionally joined the group at the Pomidor, Vadim goaded them to tell stories about the glory days of the secret city. The couple had very much enjoyed their time there and spoke of their past rather wistfully. Vadim put on a long face, but it was obvious that he was pleased that he was doing better financially than his old friend Evgeny, who had a better education and had, at least for a while, been part of the good life.

Lubov or Aleksy would occasionally bring up the nuclear subject, searching for information, being careful not to be too aggressive. After several months of subtle questioning, Lubov decided the time was right. "I wonder how much money a real nuclear weapon might be worth?" she wondered innocently. She was surprised; this group of mainly blue-collar workers had given it some serious thought, and, as usual, Vadim had an answer.

"Well, Kadafi offered some, what was it, several million American dollars a few years back, but I don't think anything became of that. But then that fat guy came through here about six months ago, sat right here in the Pomidor, and made big claims that he'd pay 10 billion rubles for nuclear material. None of us had much of a clue about that kind of stuff, didn't really like the guy and, after a few days, he didn't show up again. I wouldn't have trusted him anyway; he looked too much like a Muslim."

Aleksy, who was now known as "Professor America" and who had emerged as one of the more knowledgeable leaders of the nightly assemblage, picked up the thread. "That might be a little high, but from what I've heard, there is big money out there for almost any kind of nuclear material. There seems to be a real black market. I've talked to some of the people at school about this, and from what I've heard, the Soviet accounting system was so haphazard that many people believe there are unaccounted-for weapons just lying around in some of those abandoned facilities. Could that be possible?"

The group was divided on this, as it was on almost everything: "Sure, it's possible!" "No, of course not." The discussion went out for hours, late into the evening. More vodka than usual was consumed that night.

"You know what, hon," Lubov remarked to Aleksy as they walked home from the Pomidor a couple of evenings thereafter, "I am really beginning to like it here. If it wasn't for my lousy, pandering boss, this would be a nice place to live. Despite all their continual bitching about the government, these people are fun loving, very pleasant to be around. I've never been so happy. This would sure be a nice place to settle and raise a family."

This really frightened Aleksy; this would not work. "Are you serious, sweetheart?" Aleksy replied, alarmed that Lubov seemed to be losing focus. "Do you no longer believe in our mission?"

"Of course I do. I was just kind of daydreaming, maybe thinking to myself, I guess. But I do envy these people."

"I do, too, in a way, but we need to remember that we're here to fulfill the will of Allah. Inshallah."

"Inshallah," Lubov responded, a bit embarrassed by her revelation.

CHAPTER FOUR
Evgeny

The Pomidor conversation about the forgotten nuclear weapons was still playing in Vadim's head about a week later when he stopped at Evgeny and Lilia's to have a beer and play with the girls. These days, he mainly saw his old friends at their home since they could not afford to go out very often. They had four mouths to feed and, regardless of how hard they worked, how many extra hours they put in, their income never seemed to increase as rapidly as inflation; they just could not seem to come close to the same standard of living as they had enjoyed at Zlatoust-36.

Lilia despaired. There was so much she wanted for the girls, and it frustrated her to see Evgeny spending time on sketches of farm equipment that she suspected would never become reality. She also worried about Evgeny's perpetual restlessness; she knew that he was not happy at work and was afraid he would rather be with Vadim down at the Pomidor than spend the evening at home helping the girls with their homework and playing Durak with her. When Vadim told Evgeny about the conversation about nuclear material that they had had at the Pomidor, a strange look came over his friend's face. The more Vadim described Professor America's interest and his possible connections, the more intense Evgeny's face became. It was apparent that something had been kindled in Evgeny's mind.

"Hey, Evgeny, what is it? You know something, don't you? Do you think that there are there still nuclear weapons up there?"

"Vadim! Vadim! Slow down. I don't know. I don't remember. It's just been too long."

Evgeny knew. At least he suspected he knew. He remembered that awful period in Zlatoust in 1991 when so many of the nuclear artillery shells they had been examining failed the quality assurance inspection because of plutonium corrosion. Plutonium corrodes and expands when exposed to humidity, and since the pits were not hermetically sealed, the corrosion was severe enough to seriously degrade the shell's performance.

The Soviet authorities were not pleased with this high number of rejects and, of course, they blamed Evgeny and his fellow inspectors. To get the authorities off their backs, the inspectors devised a self-preservation strategy. Management was willing to accept one reject in every group of fifteen shells. If the inspectors found a group that had two rejects, they hid one of the offending weapons in an outlying equipment shed, adjusted the paperwork, and then reinserted the weapon back into the system when they had a clean set of fourteen shells. The system had worked admirably.

Or, it had, up until the morning of the "it's all over" announcement. Now, four years later, Evgeny remembered hiding a shell in the equipment shed earlier that morning, and he was willing to bet that in the rush to abandon the site no one had thought to retrieve that weapon from its hiding place. So, yes, Evgeny quite possibly did know where there was a nuclear weapon.

Did he want to get involved in such a dangerous, disloyal scheme, one that could harm not only him but Lilia and the girls? The money would be wonderful: he could quit his job, could build prototypes of his equipment designs, could give Lilia everything she wanted. And he knew that this was Vadim's kind of adventure; Vadim would be willing, no, anxious, to help in any endeavor Evgeny devised.

But could he do it? He had already compromised his principles by working at Zlatoust-36; could he take this additional step? Did such a scheme have a chance of working? If there was a forgotten weapon, how hard would it be to retrieve it? He had not been out to the plant since the day that everything had been abruptly shuttered. What was there now?

If he did this, he felt it would be a major act of disloyalty, a betrayal of his country. But was it really? Wasn't loyalty a two-way street? How much loyalty had the Soviet Union shown to the people of the Chelyabinsk Oblast when they had so arrogantly contaminated the entire region and then just walked away from the mess with no show of remorse and no intention of compensation?

Unsurprisingly, Vadim did not share any of Evgeny's reservations. When Evgeny finally told his friend there might be a forgotten weapon, not only was Vadim ready but was, perhaps, Evgeny thought, a bit too exuberant. Despite Evgeny's cautions, almost every time he encountered Aleksy, Vadim managed to offhandedly find a way to introduce the subject of nuclear weapons into the conversation. Aleksy, although he did not actively respond, noted the discussion with interest and suspected that, if he was reading Vadim correctly, he and Lubov might have a chance of completing their mission within the next few weeks.

One night at the Pomidor, Lubov decided the time had arrived. "Enough," she taunted Vadim. "Enough talk. If someone actually knows something about where a weapon might be, well okay, but all of this hypothetical bravado, repeating the same thing over and over, is getting boring. You're lots of talk, Vadim, but not much action. Do you really know something?" Uncharacteristically abashed, Vadim did not answer and the subject was discussed with much less frequency in the subsequent evenings.

After thinking about nothing else for several weeks, when awake and when trying to sleep, Evgeny finally decided it would not hurt anything to just take a ride out to Zlatoust-36 and do a little reconnaissance. He somewhat reluctantly recruited Vadim to join him, and Vadim made an elaborate pledge to secrecy. As worried as he was, this gesture forced Evgeny to smile; Vadim had never kept a secret in his life.

It was heartbreaking. The once-proud city had decayed and crumbled. There were no kids laughing on the playground, no people bustling about on the streets, no sounds of the city to be heard; the city had lost its soul. In a quick drive around the perimeter of the tech area, Evgeny carefully noted that the electric sensors on the fence were no longer operable and that the exterior security was now nothing more than a single five-foot high mesh wire/barbed wire fence.

As they passed the main guard gate, Evgeny spotted a familiar face. "Kayla!" he hollered in surprise and joy as he greeted an old friend in a guard's uniform, one of the two guards manning the post. "Evgeny!" Kayla exclaimed as the two men hugged and shook hands exuberantly.

"I didn't know you were still here, Kayla. Oh, it's so good to see you." After catching up on family news, Evgeny asked, "May we come inside and look around?"

"I'd love to let you but that's not permitted. I don't know why, there's really nothing left and there are only about twenty people who come up to work every day. They're supposedly cleaning up some of the old facilities, but I don't see much being shipped out. Why don't you wait around a few minutes, it's about time for the shift to end and some of your old buddies will be coming out."

"Great idea, that'll give us more time to catch up."

Kayla led Evgeny and Vadim into the guard shack. As the three men chatted about families, sports, and the changes at the plant, Evgeny and Vadim paid particular attention to Kayla's descriptions of his job and the tech area's security setup. Apparently there were three guard shifts, with four men per shift—two at the gate and two roving around the area twenty-four hours per day. On average, the roving guards checked the site perimeter twice per shift.

Fortunately, before Vadim's overly plying questions about Kayla's job elicited suspicion, some of Evgeny's old work friends made their way through the gate. He was delighted to see these men he had been so close to for so long but had not seen since the day he had left the city. They embraced him excitedly and there might have been a few tears. After about an hour of happy conversation, Evgeny and Vadim left, Evgeny warmed by renewed friendship and Vadim warmed by the laxness of Zlatoust-36's remaining security.

Vadim was at his most annoyingly animated on the ride home, and Evgeny was extra pensive. After half an hour of ignoring Vadim's chatter, Evgeny finally turned to his old friend. "I refuse to listen to any more of this. Before we discuss this again, you must find out if there's a real offer for a weapon or if it's just a bunch of talk. Then, and only then, will I think seriously about it. And if I hear you've been indiscrete and talking too much, we'll just forget that it was ever considered. Do you understand me?"

As Evgeny endlessly weighed the pros and cons of the situation, he never quite came to a definitive decision. But he always seemed to take the next step and soon found himself planning a more thorough reconnaissance trip to 36, contingent upon Vadim getting some indication of a potential purchaser. When being assigned that specific task, Vadim was exuberant. Immediately heading to the Pomidor, he excitedly waylaid Aleksy and Lubov when they arrived.

"No, don't sit down. Come on a walk with me. We have to talk in private."

As the three strolled along the riverbank, Vadim grilled the couple. "Do you believe that it's true that someone might pay as much as 10 billion rubles for a nuclear weapon?"

"That seems high to me. But three billion rubles wouldn't surprise me," Aleksy replied.

"Suppose someone had a nuclear weapon, how would he contact the people who might be interested in buying it?" Vadim pressed. "How would he know if they were trustworthy? That would really scare me."

"I don't really know," Aleksy answered, trying to look nonchalant. "But, if you're really serious, I could look into it for you. I've heard some rumblings around school. I know a couple of people who seem to know that kind of stuff."

"I don't know, Aleksy. Even that would be frightening to me," Vadim responded. "If I had a nuclear weapon, I'd be hesitant to do business with someone I didn't know. I don't think I could do that."

"Neither could I, Vadim. But I sense that we've progressed past just speaking hypothetically, right? Ideally, if I consulted my sources and found a purchaser, then Lubov and I could act as emissaries if you'd like, and the deal would actually be between you and us. That way Lubov and I could also make a few rubles. All the risk would be on our side—we'd be the ones taking the chance that the purchaser was trustworthy, not you. Let me check around. Now let's get back to the Pomidor. I suspect there is some vodka waiting for us."

Several evenings later Lubov appeared at the Pomidor alone. She asked Vadim to take a walk with her. Amid catcalls—Vadim's reputation as a womanizer was never far from anyone's mind, and Lubov was an exceedingly attractive woman—the pair left the cafe.

"Aleksy has spoken with someone who knows a person who might be willing to buy a nuclear weapon. The buyer will need to know more about it before he can make an offer. Aleksy drove this afternoon to Miass to talk to him, to see if he's really interested, and if so, to make the preliminary arrangements to get a portion of the money to prove their sincerity. He would like to get some of it right away and the remainder when the deal is done. Does that seem okay? Now Vadim, we need for you to be completely up front with us: can you really produce a weapon? This is for real, risks are being taken; if you are just talking, we need to know now."

"I wouldn't be asking these questions if we weren't serious. But before we proceed any further, I need to check with my partners," Vadim responded, his heart racing. Maybe this was going to happen! "But you may tell your associate that the weapon is a Russian 152mm artillery shell."

Within a few days, Evgeny agreed to the offer of three billion rubles, and Vadim relayed the decision to Lubov. Evgeny managed to convince himself that he had made the right decision, rationalizing that it was not really a betrayal because the Russian government had long-since broken its covenant with the people of the Chelyabinsk Oblast. It was not until the next week, when he and Vadim were staring at the 500 million ruble down payment, that he began to realize the trouble that he would be in if the weapon was not where it had been left that January morning four years earlier.

• • •

Apprehension was far too mild a word to describe Evgeny's state of mind as they approached the outer barrier to his former workplace. Evgeny had never been outside the tech area's security fence at night, and even though all he and Vadim were doing was scouting out where they might attack the security system, Evgeny found himself quivering. It would be less frightening if Vadim would stop the incessant questioning and just let him think. He had been doing a lot of thinking. In the time that had elapsed since this adventure began, he had replayed the day that the plant had closed over and over in his mind and could not image which plant manager or individual might have discovered that weapon. Every time, the answer came back as "no one," but still the fear would not go away.

The two men held their breath as the guards passed by. Thankfully, the guards seemed far more interested in the music playing on their radio than they did in inspecting the fence. Evgeny had calculated that they should have about four hours before the patrol came around again.

As soon as the guards were out of sight, Evgeny and Vadim hustled across the road and through the ten-meter ditch of overgrown weeds. Evgeny carefully inspected the fence and located and showed Vadim the exact spot where they could penetrate the security system.

"Why here? Couldn't we just crawl over the fence? Do we need to get another guy for a lookout, Aleksy for example?" Vadim's litany of questions continued. Evgeny remained silent, hurrying back to the car, motioning Vadim to hurry up and join him.

On the drive back from Zlatoust, Evgeny silently reflected on the scheme; he had not seen anything that had led him to believe retrieving the weapon would be more difficult than he had initially suspected, assuming of course that the weapon remained where they had placed it years ago.

He was still not entirely comfortable with his plan. While he had little doubt that they could gain access to the building, there was no way of knowing the likelihood of their getting through the doors, retrieving the weapon, and escaping without detection. And, should they be caught, he had been unable to come up with any believable explanation for their presence. They were working without a safety net. But things had progressed too far to back out now; there was no way to replace the money that he had already spent.

Evgeny had used part of his share of the earnest money to open savings accounts for each of the girls and a sizeable portion of the rest to do something that Lilia had nagged him about for months: he took out a life insurance policy. He had been considering buying life insurance ever since Eugenia was born but had never felt he had enough money. Now there was a more compelling reason: he was about to embark on something that could prove exceedingly dangerous; not only the danger of the act itself but also because he was feeling less and less comfortable with the relationship between Vadim and his "Professor America."

When he played everything over in his mind, something about the weapon turnover process also bothered him. It just seemed too ill defined, too vague and tenuous, a typical Vadim plan. When Evgeny pressed Vadim for more details, all he could get were noncommittal answers like, "I don't really know, I'll talk to Aleksy about it tonight, we're working on it." When he questioned

Vadim about how the rest of the money was to be delivered, it was the same thing: "Let me talk to Aleksy about it." These vague answers didn't reassure Evgeny, but they weren't reason enough to call everything off.

Evgeny's biggest fear was that Vadim's loquaciousness would compromise the operation. Vadim held court at the Pomidor almost every night with tales of triumph; Evgeny feared that there was no way he could resist boasting about an escapade of this magnitude.

Evgeny was also suspicious of Aleksy's repeated insistence on accompanying them when they went to retrieve the weapon. "No way," Evgeny told Vadim. "If he keeps pressuring you, tell him that the whole deal is off." Aleksy finally relented but, through Vadim, was continually trying to solicit more details of their impending plan than the uneasy Evgeny thought was necessary.

Evgeny rehearsed and modified the plan of attack until he was confident that what he had come up with was as good as possible with the information he had. He kept the details from Vadim—better to deal with Vadim on a need-to-know basis.

It was necessary to discuss the contingency plan with Vadim. If the guards discovered them, the last thing Evgeny wanted was to be confronted with a flood of questions from Vadim. The contingency plan was simple: both he and Vadim would carry a military flash-bang grenade. If they were detected, they would run in opposite directions and each throw his grenade as far as possible to divert their pursuers. With the minimal staffing at the site, perhaps only one of them would be caught. Evgeny had considered having them both carry pistols but discarded the idea because there was no way he could shoot former friends; he sternly warned the irrepressible Vadim that if he chose to arm himself, the entire operation would be cancelled.

True to Evgeny's technical training and his belief in operational simplicity, there was nothing complicated about the plan. They would wait for a new moon, cut a hole in the fence, dash for the cover of the building, cut the padlock, force open the sliding sheet metal door, retrieve the shell, transport it in a blanket they would bring with them, and dash back to their car. The greatest problem, he felt, was in being detected during entry. If this happened there would probably be a whole phalanx of guards assembled outside of the door awaiting their departure: making them sitting ducks, as the saying goes.

• • •

As the date for the operation approached, Evgeny could not shake his unease about Aleksy. One night at the Pomidor, Aleksy and Lubov made several allusions to the upcoming operation, suggesting to Evgeny that they knew too much about the plan. Evgeny almost blew up when Vadim loudly joined the conversation, but he worked to control his anger; now more than ever both he and Vadim needed to be calm. He decided that it was just nerves making him so sensitive. The first rule for any operation was to make a good plan and stick to it. He had made a good plan.

As a cover, he told Lilia he was going to spend a few days hiking in the mountains with Vadim, something they had enjoyed quite a bit when they were growing up. Lilia was not overjoyed at the prospect; she still feared Vadim could be a bad influence on Evgeny, but she hoped a few days of hiking and fishing would help him shake his lingering melancholy and restlessness.

"What a wonderful idea," she said, even managing to feign a bit of enthusiasm.

Evgeny and Vadim headed out toward their favorite hiking trail from the old days, a trail that originated near the base of Mt. Zavjalikha, a short distance from Trekhgorny.

Approaching the trailhead, Evgeny announced, "Don't unload all the stuff just yet, I'd like to hike just a short way up, come back, and go after that weapon tonight rather than tomorrow."

"What? Why?" Vadim stammered, clearly surprised.

"I'm not sure; I guess I'd just like to get it over with as soon as possible. Do you see any problem with getting the thing tonight and then hiding out for a day? We'll have plenty of opportunities to go fishing after we're rich."

"No, I really can't see a problem. I'm ready whenever you are. I like the thought of being rich!"

They were in place shortly after dark. They hid the car in an abandoned shed and then carefully moved themselves and their equipment to a secluded spot near the edge of the residential area where they could observe the peripheral fence. After an interminable wait, the lackadaisical guard patrol came past, barely glancing at the fence, eating their lunches while in deep conversation.

Evgeny and Vadim ran to the fence. Evgeny snipped a hole in the wire mesh and the two men crawled through. They paused for a moment, listening for any noise that might indicate they had been observed. Hearing nothing, they crept slowly through the weeds and abandoned debris to the rear of the building, keeping low and stopping intermittently to listen. The only sound was their own frightened breathing.

The sudden frantic squawking and wing-beating of a bird roused from its sleep froze both men in mid-stride; without communication they dropped to the ground, both fighting the temptation to turn and run. They waited, but no lights came on, and there were no loud, alarmed voices.

They stood, glanced at each other for assurance, and resumed their journey, creeping around to the front of the building. Evgeny removed the bolt cutters from his tool vest and easily cut through the steel shaft of the padlock. Very gently they pushed on the sliding door. Nothing. Applying more force, they broke it loose. The door screeched as it slid, perhaps for the first time in four years. The men dropped to the ground, but nothing happened. They waited a little longer; still nothing.

They stood slowly and then carefully slid the door open enough to enter. Making arcs through the eerie darkness, the beams from their flashlights revealed the scurrying noises belonged to scores of rats searching for hiding places. Evgeny and Vadim slowly moved through the jumble of old, discarded machines to the small room in the rear. Finally, their flashlights illuminated a tarp that looked familiar to Evgeny. The two men lifted the tarp. Dislodged vermin ran for cover, but Evgeny and Vadim had eyes only for the beautiful, dusty 152 mm artillery shell resting beneath the tarp.

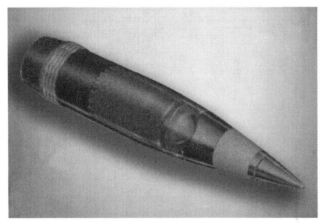

Nuclear Artillery Shell

Vadim started to say something, but Evgeny silenced him with a look. They silently began to carefully work the transport blanket under the forty-five kilogram shell. Once the blanket was securely under the shell, they dragged their prize toward the entrance door of the windowless structure.

As they moved forward, Vadim stopped. "Did you hear that?"

Evgeny set his side of the load down and listened, shaking his head. Then he heard it: the unmistakable wail of a police vehicle, the frequency of the siren increasing as the vehicle approached. Evgeny and Vadim looked at each other in dismay. They laid the weapon down and started toward the door, digging the diversionary grenades out of their backpacks. As they approached the door, the frequency and intensity of the siren began decreasing until it disappeared in the distance; apparently, this bell did not toll for them. So they hoped.

Returning to the weapon, they continued their journey, setting the shell down as they reached the door. Evgeny prayed silently before sliding the door slightly ajar, opening it further when he did not see anyone. He motioned Vadim to follow him, sliding the weapon over the threshold. Again they paused, almost not believing they had not been detected.

Moving as quietly as possible, they returned to the fence, slid the weapon and themselves through the hole, grabbed the straps that had been sewn on to the corners of the blanket, and ran across the open area to the temporary location they had chosen to hide the weapon. When they reached the protected area and paused to catch their breath, they looked at each other with utter amazement.

For once Vadim had nothing to say. Neither could truly believe that they had been successful; they just sat there in the darkness in disbelief and self-satisfaction.

Finally it was too much for Vadim; he broke the silence with a whoop. "By God, we did it! I can't believe we actually did it!"

Evgeny tried to silence him. "Quiet, damn it, we're not home yet."

"But we're rich, Evgeny! We're rich!"

"Come on," Evgeny growled. "Go get the car and let's finish this. Then we'll go up in the mountains and you can shout all you want."

Vadim picked his way through the dark and still-sleeping town, retrieved his car, and managed to find his way back to Evgeny. He opened the hatchback and the two again lifted the shell and gingerly set it down in the trunk. Closing the lid, they turned around to find themselves facing two black-clad figures, each holding what was recognizable in the dim light as a Markov pistol.

Evgeny and Vadim's animal-ravaged bodies were found by hikers late the following spring in a ravine on the north side of Mt. Zavjalikha. Russian police had been trying to solve the missing persons case for months. They had interviewed Vadim's cronies at the Pomidor but had been unable to find Aleksy and Lubov.

No wonder. By the time the police began to conduct interviews, the couple had delivered the weapon to their associate in Miass and were back at their base camp in northern Sudan, enjoying the praise and admiration of their comrades.

CHAPTER FIVE
Mose

"Sure, I like Paris," Mose found himself saying to anyone who asked. "All except for the Parisians." Paris in September was beautiful. He did not know why he was leading the Takfir team in the French capital, but he was flattered that the Command Council had chosen him. He suspected the decision was made, at least partially, to reward him for the success of his pupils Masud and Minifu.

He was worried about the assignment. He was not at all sure he could find the perfect place in Paris to position the nuclear weapon without attracting the attention of the local authorities. And the Command Council seemed completely uninterested in providing him with the assistance he requested.

The mission unfolded quickly. When Masud and Minifu returned to the Sudan after successfully delivering the weapon to their associate in Miass, there was revelry—eating, drinking, and dancing— for two full days. Then, abruptly, the celebrations ended. Tense, high-level discussions among the leaders began, and from what Mose could determine as he hovered close to the Command Post, there were two streams of thought dividing the Takfir Command Council.

One group wanted to avenge all past grievances by detonating the weapon and killing as many infidels as possible; the other group was more interested in embarrassing the so-called major powers on the world stage by extorting them, showing them that Islamic fundamentalists were more than a bunch of uneducated "rag heads." This approach would not necessarily require the detonation of the weapon and, its proponents argued, could position them with better moral standing in the world community.

Mose strongly favored the second course of action, feeling that either choice made the same statement but that the less lethal approach would be met with greater acceptance by both the Muslim and non-Muslim worlds. He was quite pleased when rumors began to indicate that it was the latter path that was being chosen.

He was also pleased to be called before the council to present his views on the situation. He recommended making the operation as uncluttered as possible: place the weapon in its final destination and use it as a bargaining chip. The council thanked him, acknowledged him for his training efforts that resulted in the securing of the weapon, and dismissed him from the deliberations.

Two days later he was called back to the assemblage. The council informed him that his advice had so impressed them that his recommendations were being incorporated into the plan of action. This pleased him, but the next piece of news terrified him: the council members were highly impressed by his resume, so impressed that they were naming him leader of the weapon emplacement team. Within days he was going to travel halfway around the world with a nuclear weapon, and he knew precisely nothing about nuclear weapons.

• • •

His training started immediately. When the device arrived in the Sudan, it was housed in a recently completed climate-controlled hospital facility. A concertina wire-topped barricade had been erected around the facility, and twenty-four-hour sentries were established. When the council decided on its plan of action, twenty scientists, engineers, and technicians arrived from Egypt. The Egyptians were in charge of cleaning up and modifying the weapon and teaching Mose enough about the rudiments of nuclear weaponry for him to complete his mission and deal with any unexpected contingencies.

Mose was amazed at the loving care the scientists bestowed on the shell.

The head scientist, Sharif, an old acquaintance of Mose's, tried to explain the basics of nuclear weaponry to him. "To get a nuclear yield, we've got to worry about the simultaneity of the compression, about neutrons being present at the proper time, about our being in control of the device so that it will detonate when we want it to. You watch, and we'll attempt to explain as we go along. But it's going to be a slow process, and you'd better be prepared to learn. And even though all of these guys have spent years working around high explosives, the modifications they're going to make to get it ready are going to be dangerous, particularly so out here in the field."

First, the scientists carefully disassembled the shell. They removed the nose cone, taking out the contact fuse that would no longer be needed. This exposed the front end of the high explosive (HE) shell and an unusual-looking detonator. Next they broke loose the aft joint, the joint between the section of the shell containing the warhead and the rear/rotating band section that housed the neutron generator and the other electronic components. These two parts did not separate easily, requiring more pounding, drilling, and profanity than Mose would have preferred. Finally it broke loose, and the sections were pulled apart, exposing a detonator in the rear of the HE that was identical to the one in the front. Mose had worked a little around explosives, but these detonators were different than anything he had previously seen.

Sharif observed his astonishment. "They're EBWs, exploding bridge wire detonators, and they're necessary to achieve the simultaneity I just mentioned. With this type of detonator, the weapon explosive is initiated by a shockwave rather than by heat alone. With the hot-wire initiator, which you are used to, the initiation is not sufficiently simultaneous to achieve the necessary symmetrical compression of the plutonium."

Mose turned his head to watch the scientists attempting to remove the front detonator from the shell, having concluded that he might be in over his head and wondering if he was getting far more information than he actually needed to know.

But Sharif was not letting him off the hook yet. He moved back into Mose's view and continued. "We're concerned with the conditions of those detonators and would like to replace them. We've managed to get a whole box of EBWs smuggled in from the United States. We'd like to replace those that are currently in the weapon. If you'll come in closer, you can see that they're badly corroded."

Sharif stopped talking as they both turned to watch the technician struggling to free the uncooperative detonator. Unsuccessful and cursing, the agitated technician discontinued wrestling with the recalcitrant detonator and moved to the opposite end of the shell. Several attempts to remove the other detonator met with an equal lack of success.

"I'm simply afraid to put more torque on them," he announced to the crowd surrounding the device. "If I break them off, we're going to be in a shitload of trouble, and I'll probably have to drill them out. We might be able to loosen them with some solvent if you'd like. Would anyone like to make a suggestion?"

No one offered. After consultation amongst themselves, the scientists concluded that using solvent was not desirable and that it was probably best just to leave the original detonators in the device and hope that their performance was not degraded by the deterioration.

"Did you see the neutron generator when they separated it from the firing set?" Sharif asked Mose. "Unfortunately, we don't have a replacement, so we're going to have to use that one and hope it still works. Neutron generators all tend to degrade with time, but we really don't have much choice—it's a one-shot device, so we can't even test it."

"Hold on a minute, Sharif. You're talking to me—Mose, the street fighter. I'm sure what you're explaining is important, but I don't even know what a neutron generator is, why it's needed, or what it's for." Mose was irritated, his sense of inadequacy growing by the minute.

Sharif grinned just a bit. "I'm sorry, Mose, you're right. I was going way too fast. Why the neutron generator? At the instance that the high explosive compresses the plutonium to about half its original size, there need to be neutrons present to trigger the nuclear reaction. What that device does is flood the region with neutrons at the appropriate time. So we're going to have to assume that their timing system is still reliable and that it will fire the generator at the proper time."

"Are we going to be able to use their firing system?"

"Unfortunately, no. In its intended use, when the shell is fired from a gun tube, the firing set receives a signal from the fuse that it's time to act when the projectile approaches its target. The firing set then charges, starts the neutron generator timer, and then fires the detonators. In our case, we're going to activate the system ourselves. We will fire the device either from the timer that we insert into the weapon or by a remote radio transmitter. We also want to retain the option of turning the device off should the French government meet our demands. Since the weapon is being used for a different purpose than its design intent, we need different firing components. The scientists claim that they have brought all of the necessary replacement components with them; I'm skeptical but we shall see. One thing that we have going for us is that we don't have the same weight and size limitations that exist when you're trying to cram all of this stuff into the one hundred and fifty-two millimeter shell envelope."

Sharif paused, watching a look of complete exasperation, almost despair, cross Mose's face. "You don't understand very much of this, do you? I'm sorry, but there's no way of predicting what problems you might encounter when you field the shell. You really do need to know this stuff, and I really need to teach you."

Mose glanced toward Sharif, a bit of anger flashing across his face. "And I don't know how to comprehend all of it in the time we have. I'm just worried that I'm going to screw something up. I've never heard of most of this stuff and now I'm supposed to understand it well enough to make corrections if something doesn't work. I think maybe you've got the wrong guy."

"Tell you what," Sharif answered. "After dinner, the rest of them are going to go back to the lab to try to get the firing system squared away. You and I will stay right here and go through the process as many times as it takes for you to become comfortable with it. Perhaps a few diagrams might make it easier to understand. Then we'll put together a checklist so you'll have a step-by-step procedure to follow when it's time to arm the weapon. If we get through all of that, then perhaps I'll let you buy me a beer or two."

Mose permitted himself to smile. "I'd really appreciate that. Are you sure we shouldn't have the beer first?"

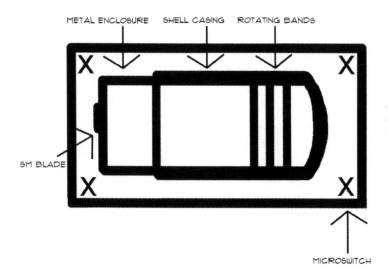

Sharif's Sketch of Shell in Shipping Container

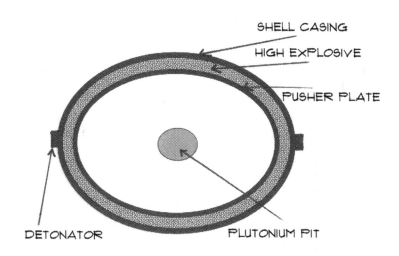

Sharif's Sketch: Cross Section of Nuclear Component of Artillery Round

By the time he finally went to bed that evening, Mose felt much more at ease; he was not sure if it was due to the enhanced understanding of the weapon or the several beers he and Sharif had shared.

When Mose returned to the lab the next morning, the team was beginning to mate the replacement components they had readied the night before with the nuclear assembly and were getting the complete package ready to ship. Sneaking a peek at the disassembled weapon, all Mose could see were the spherical ends of the explosive, tightly encased within the steel shell. The plutonium itself was not visible as it was entirely surrounded by the HE shell. The day before, he had heard the scientists discussing the possibility of taking gamma or X-ray images of the pit to see if there was detectable corrosion of the plutonium. Apparently they had decided against it, succumbing to the realization that there was not much that they could do about it even if corrosion was evident.

One problem that did require attention was the several prominent cracks visible in the end caps of the explosive, some of which looked to be far more serious than mere surface crazing. While the consensus was that these probably would not interfere substantially with the symmetry of the compression, they were still a potential safety problem; even relatively insensitive explosives can self-initiate when adjacent surfaces abrade one another during transport.

Very carefully, the explosives technician filled these cracks with Semtex, all the while muttering to himself about the unnecessary job he had been asked to do.

Finally it was time to reassemble the weapon, securing the central and rear sections of the shell together, and mating them with a massive set of batteries, the new firing set, and control system, and then attaching a pre-formed metal casing to the front of the shell covering these new components, finally affixing the entire assembly to a small wooden pallet.

After everything had been securely strapped to the pallet, the whole assembly was lowered into its protective wooden crate. The technicians positioned micro-switch devices on the bottom of the cover and the interior walls of the crate; if someone attempted to dismantle or move the crate after it was armed, these devices would trigger the internal firing sequence and the weapon would detonate. Next they inserted a long, flat polyethylene rod through a slit in the front of the crate. This was another safety device, one they referred to as the "SM blade." When the rod was in position, it isolated the batteries from the rest of the system; when removed, the circuit became operational.

As they went through this reassembly process, each of the scientists, sometimes singly, sometimes several at once, reminded Mose of the things he had to remember when activating the weapon, particularly to make sure all the micro-switches were in the safe condition before he replaced the top of the box. Each of them individually reviewed the checklist Sharif had composed, adding to, deleting, or altering list items. He essentially had the list memorized and could sense that his inquisitors were gradually becoming more confident in his capability.

One thing continued to puzzle him: why they all seemed to laugh a bit every time someone mentioned the SM blade. "Just what does SM stand for anyway?" he finally asked.

"SM," Sharif replied, "stands for Save Mose."

Mose did not find this as funny as the rest of the group did. "And what if something malfunctions when I pull the SM rod?"

"Don't worry, you'll never know it," came the reply, which Mose also failed to find funny.

With the SM rod now inserted the modification of the device was complete, and the next phase of the operation began.

•   •   •

Within days Mose found himself alone in Paris looking for the perfect place to stage the incident. It needed to be somewhere that, when discovered, would frighten people, somewhere that the consequences could be horrifying. He was in daily contact with his controller and was greatly relieved to find out that personnel assistance would arrive with the weapon.

"Don't worry," the controller reassured him, "you'll have plenty of help when you need it. Right now we're busy trying to find a secure place to store the weapon when it arrives from Le Havre."

Mose did not know the actual path the weapon had taken to France, but he knew it would arrive by ship in Le Havre, packed inside a transport container filled with expensive Oriental rugs. If things went as planned, it would be secreted out of the transport container at a dockside warehouse, arrive in Paris by hearse, and stored until he was ready for it.

Mose spent several days scouting for a site in Paris. His efforts pleased him, but it surprised him that he was beginning to feel lonely. In the past, he had spent many solitary days on sentry duty, but somehow the beauty of Paris cried to be shared. There were hundreds of thousands of Muslims in Paris, most from North Africa, and some were former friends and acquaintances. He was reluctant to contact these former associates for fear that the reason for his presence in the city might be questioned and discovered. He had intentionally located lodging in a predominantly student section of the city, on the Left Bank, in order to distance himself from the Muslim community. But while his loneliness was principally of his own making, it was also real.

He remembered how changed Masud and Minifu had seemed when they returned from Russia. They were no longer dogmatic zealots; in fact, Minifu told him, she now thought that it might be easier to accomplish some of their religious and political goals through cooperation with people of other faiths. This had shocked Mose when he first heard it, but now he understood the change in his compatriots. It was surprisingly difficult to remain fervently anti-West while in the West. Without his colleagues continually reinforcing their hatred of all things anti-Muslim, Mose began to question whether he was still willing to die for the cause. He knew he no longer possessed the unquestioning desire to kill hundreds of the unknowing, phony infidels—he was having trouble believing that was Allah's will. He did still believe that they deserved to be taught a painful lesson; they needed to realize that the Arabs were not an inferior race, and that the Western world's arrogance and air of superiority toward people of Arabian descent would prove to be an expensive lesson for them.

His scouting led him to believe that the best place for the weapon was the system of tunnels that underlie virtually all of Paris. He had been told that the most interesting of these tunnels were the catacombs, so he decided to see for himself, entering the public entrance across the street from the Denfert-Rochereau Metro station. He had done his research: he knew the tunnels were part of an excavated manmade quarry system and that they ran for nearly two hundred miles. Late in the eighteenth century, enterprising Parisians, running out of empty space for aboveground cemeteries, had turned the tunnels into a necropolis for approximately six million deceased citizens. Supposedly included in this massive grave were such notables as Robespierre and Madame de Pompadour, their unidentified bones carefully stacked along the walls of the caverns with the remains of a multitude of their fellow Parisians. This series of passages were only the upper layer of the tunnels that ran under most of the city, while below them were the sewer system and the tunnels dug for the Rapid Transit Rail lines.

Entering the catacombs, Mose was immediately discouraged. It would be impossible to carry the bulky weapon down the spiral staircase that descended to the floor of the sixty-five-meter cavern. Dejected, he turned around to leave, but the continual flow of incoming traffic on the staircase made a quick exit impossible, so he trudged onward. He had heard that the tour took less than an hour, so the easiest course was just to continue. After about a fifteen minute walk in the rather chilly, narrow, dimly lit tunnel, he and his chattering group of twenty tourists encountered a sign that brought absolute silence: "Arrete! C'est ici l'empire de la mort." "Stop! This is the empire of death."

When the slow-moving group stopped to hear the guide's narration, Mose kept walking. The tour guide, perhaps dismayed at the loss of a potential tip,

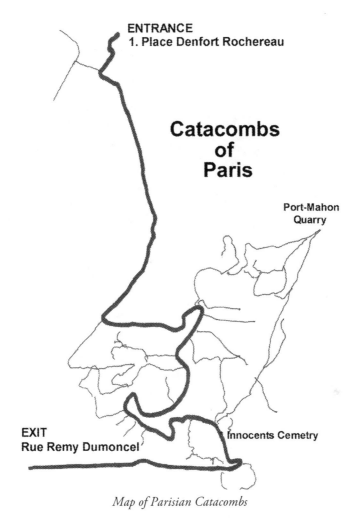

ENTRANCE
1. Place Denfort Rochereau

Catacombs of Paris

Port-Mahon
Quarry

EXIT
Rue Remy Dumoncel

Innocents Cemetry

Map of Parisian Catacombs

perhaps because he saw himself as the boss of the catacombs, yelled after Mose, warning him of the number of visitors who had been lost forever in the catacombs. Mose thanked him and proceeded, not wanting to waste any more time or to appear in any of the photographs that were being flashed almost continuously by his group of Japanese tourists.

Racing on ahead, he quickly took pictures of some of the crypts and the artfully stacked bones. It was truly amazing! Femur bones created walls that were two meters high and, in some places, more than five meters deep. He found several areas that would work very well for his purposes if, somehow, the weapon could be squeezed down that spiral staircase and through the narrow tunnels. Within fifteen minutes he had passed a dozen monuments,

51

crypts, and galleries of bones from specific churches. The walls of many of the larger caverns were buttressed and braced; some had actually been sprayed with liquid concrete to keep the limestone, sand, and clay on top of the catacombs in place, precluding an accidental visit from the still-living citizens of Paris.

Bones lining wall of Catacombs

Mose was sure he was getting close to the exit, as he had been inside for about an hour, when he came across the chamber of the Cemetery of Innocents. He could not believe it: this was the perfect site for his mission! It was a large, well-reinforced cavern ten meters or so in height and equally wide. Mose took about a dozen pictures before quickly continuing when he heard his tour group and the aggrieved guide quickly approaching. Turning the corner, he found himself in another long, narrow tunnel with a paved floor and a gentle upward slope. The tunnel led up a few shallow steps to a metal door, which, when he pushed it open, exited right out onto the Rue Remy Dumoncel.

"Blessed be Allah," Mose whispered to himself. "This will really work." He could see that it would be possible to bring the device in through the exit door, carry it the forty meters or so down the tunnel and around the first corner, and right into the Innocents cemetery. His search for the location to emplace the weapon was over.

His controller gave his unqualified approval to the choice of site later that evening. The controller and Mose discussed further plans for the operation: when the weapon would be emplaced, what equipment and documents would need to be generated, and how many people would be required. Mose was told that the weapon was not yet in Paris and that he should just lay low and enjoy the city until they were ready to proceed.

Exhilarated when he left the meeting, Mose was hit by a renewed wave of loneliness as he approached his lodgings. He had no one to celebrate his success with, and all he could look forward to was an empty apartment and another solitary, warmed-up dinner. Once again, his thoughts turned inexorably to Minifu. Mose had enjoyed the company of many women in his day, but it was Minifu, the feisty Minifu, who currently captured his imagination.

Determined not to succumb to self-pity, he took the Metro to one of the exuberant bistros on Saint Germaine and enjoyed a wonderful meal, too much cheap French wine, and the company of a group of raucous university students. He was not sure how or when he got home, but he was relieved the next morning when he opened his eyes to discover that he was alone.

Once the burden of finding the hiding place was off his shoulders, Mose enjoyed Paris. He basked in the sunshine while sitting at a sidewalk cafe reading the morning newspaper, spent a whole day in the Louvre, and even took a trip to Monet's home and gardens at Giverny. When a week elapsed without a word from his controller, he began to wonder if something had gone severely wrong, either with the shipment or their plans.

Finally the call came. He arrived at the prearranged meeting place well before the designated time of 9:00 pm. Not wanting to call attention to himself by hovering around the door of the boarded-up storefront where the meeting was to take place, he walked into one of the immaculate Parisian parks across the street and sat down on one of the cold metal benches. He was just beginning to enjoy the crisp, fall evening when he noticed her approaching, her spiked heels clicking on the concrete walk, her hips swaying suggestively.

"Would you like some company, handsome?" she asked.

"No, no, no. Please leave, I'm waiting for someone," he stammered, waving her off with his arms. How degrading, how utterly disgusting, he thought. What a depraved society this was. There was no longer any doubt in his mind: destroying the West could well be Allah's will.

• • •

Admitted to the abandoned slaughterhouse at exactly nine, he could make out four figures in the dim setting at the rear of the shop. As his eyes acclimated, he recognized his controller, but not any of the others.

"Mose, over here," a voice said in the darkness.

"Jawwad? Jawwad, is that you?" Mose replied, squinting into the darkness, recognizing the voice of one of technicians he had worked with in the desert as they got the weapon ready to ship.

"Mose!" Jawwad exclaimed as he stepped forward and the two men embraced. "We've got good news. The weapon is here, here in Paris. We're free to proceed whenever you are ready. My team and I will help you move and set up the weapon."

Mose was delighted to see Jawwad. He recognized that his friend's presence might suggest the council did not have complete confidence in his ability to arm the device once it was in place, but that did not matter. Having Jawwad here meant the responsibility was not his alone. He was no longer all by himself.

As they sat around in the dark, musty shop, Mose learned what had been happening.

Jawwad and his accomplices had managed to bribe their way onto the freighter that brought the weapon to Le Havre. Then they carefully observed as the transport container filled with carpets and the weapon had been offloaded and sealed in a dockside warehouse. With the assistance of a sizeable number of francs, the weapon was extracted from its hiding place and secreted in the hearse that was standing by. The container holding the device had been under Jawwad's team's surveillance from the time it left the desert until it reached its current resting place.

The council had decided that Mose should insert the weapon into the catacombs the following evening. He watched in amazement as the controller unboxed four sets of official l'Ossuaire Municipal workman's coveralls, complete with credentials that identified the wearers as museum employees. In addition, he gave Mose a key to unlock the rear door on Rue Remy Dumoncel, and paperwork to adhere to the crate, designating it as the base for a new altar to be erected in the Cemetery of Innocents. He promised that when they picked it up, the crate would be heavily stenciled with the phrases Fragile, Do Not Move, and Do Not Touch. Shortly after midnight the next night, four of them would carry the crate though the exit door, down the tunnel, and into the Innocents chamber. If they were accosted by one of the periodic roving guards, they were to show him the paperwork. If he accepted it, fine, if not, he would have to be convinced.

• • •

The next night there was nobody in sight when they arrived at the exit door. While one of Jawwad's colleagues moved the car around the corner, Mose opened the unalarmed door, and they moved the crate inside. With the team reassembled, the steps proved to be no problem and they soon found themselves at the Innocents site.

Mose removed from his pocket the detailed checklist he had carefully secreted since Sharif had first prepared it back in the desert. The men followed the list, point by point: removing the cover and packing material, confirming that nothing had been damaged during shipment, checking the power supplies. Everything was going according to plan. Next they assembled the system that would enable them to control the device from outside of the catacombs, hooking up the directional antenna to its power supply. They then hid an ultra-small receiver/transmitter into a crevice in the exit tunnel and another in a small hole they carved out in the limestone adjacent to the jamb of the exit door.

Taking a transmitter with him, Mose left the chamber, went across the street, and pushed the key to transmit the coded, high frequency signal. The technician stationed near the door signaled him that the system had indeed triggered the weapon's receiver.

This was all taking longer than they had anticipated. There were eerie noises in the catacombs at night, but as of yet, no roving guards. The operation stopped several times because they heard noises: people talking, classical music playing, bone piles disassembling—the emanations from six million souls—and they were getting spooked.

Then they heard footsteps, real ones. They slid the top back on the box just as the pair of tunnel police emerged from the chamber of Saint Laurent. The police were startled to see anyone there at that time of the day and pulled up short.

"What are you guys doing here?" they asked, slowly recognizing from the uniforms that these were museum employees. "You're working a bit past your usual quitting time, aren't you? Are you making up for an extra long tea break this afternoon?"

Mose laughed with them and handed them the museum authorization papers. "Someone's collected more francs from their parishioners to build yet another altar," Mose told them. "It's much easier doing this off-hours when we don't have tourists mingling around, taking pictures, and wanting to help; we'll be gone in a half hour or so."

"No problem, be sure you lock up when you leave. You do have a key, don't you?"

Mose retrieved the key from his pocket and showed it to them, and the satisfied guards continued their conversation, talking over the latest sexual scandal in the premier's office.

Waiting until they heard the guards close the door, Mose's team continued down the checklist, making sure that the crate was solidly positioned, using shims to level and secure it. When they finished running through the complete list, Jawwad looked at Mose, and Mose exited once more for the final communications check. As he did so, there stood the two policemen, having a final smoke before returning to the patrol room.

"Everything all right?" the taller of the two asked.

"Needed to get some fresh air, that smell down there gets to you."

"Yeah, me too," one of the policemen replied as they headed up Rue Remy Dumoncel. "I don't know how you guys can stand it for such a long time."

Mose nodded, stopped quivering, reached into his pocket, triggered the transmitter, and reentered the tunnel. Ascertaining that everything had worked properly, Jawwad placed a thin plastic painters' drop cloth over the contents of the crate to protect against the humidity, hooked up the motion sensor switches, and replaced the top of the crate. The next-to-last item on the checklist was to remove the safing device, the SM rod. Silently praying to Allah that everything was set correctly, Mose slowly withdrew the rod. Silence, beautiful, beautiful silence. No detonation! He turned and smiled at his cohorts.

The last item on the list was to leave, quickly. This they did without hesitation and without looking back. No one spoke. They locked the door behind them. The weapon was armed.

Paris was under siege.

PART TWO

One Long Afternoon

CHAPTER ONE
Saturday, September 9, 1995
Jean Denis

"Mon Dieu," the handsome, somewhat debonair, dark-haired man muttered to himself as he hurried down the Rue de la Cite. While slight in stature, Jean Denis Guilleron somehow radiated competence, intelligence, and humor.

It was 8:00 pm on a beautiful September evening in Paris, and if he'd had his way, he and Christine would be finishing their aperitifs at their favorite cafe before making their way home for a quiet dinner. Instead, he was entering the Incident Command Center in the incongruously opulent Prefecture de Police facility on the Isle de Cite, reluctantly entering a room buzzing with bureaucrats. Not his preferred way to spend a Saturday evening, particularly since it was going to be a very long evening, one that promised to turn into several long days. Just two hours earlier, a mysterious wooden crate had been found in the Crypt of the Innocents in the catacombs. It almost certainly contained a plutonium-bearing nuclear weapon.

The first email had arrived at 8:00 pm that morning at a substation of the Paris Prefecture. "A nuclear weapon, under our control, resides in Paris," it read. "It is set to detonate at the start of evening prayers on Wednesday. It will destroy a sizeable portion of your city. You do have an option. We will send our demands this afternoon. If you meet them, your city will be saved. Allah Akbar."

France had a long, sometimes uneasy relationship with Muslims. After World War II, millions of people immigrated to France from North Africa, drawn to the nation because of the legacy of past colonization and by familiarity with France's languages and customs. By 1990, there were 8 million Muslims in France, many poor and disenfranchised. There had been displays of civil unrest involving Muslims for decades, and there had also been fake nuclear threats from various Islamic groups. So when the email was immediately forwarded to the directorate of judicial police, the directorate was interested but not alarmed.

When the next email came, three hours later, to a prefecture in the fourteenth arrondissement, the interest heightened. This missive demanded that the United States release the World Trade Center bombing suspects Mohammed Salameh, Ahmud Mohammed Ajay, and Nidal Ayyad from prison; that the United Kingdom return the Rosetta Stone from the British Museum to Egypt; and that the Louvre return the statues of Ramesses II and Nakhthorheb to Cairo. In addition, the email demanded fifty million French francs. Once these conditions were met, the nuclear weapon would be disarmed. The French police were given a phone number to call in eight hours for more information.

When the call was placed, the Arabic-inflected voice that answered informed the listeners that the bomb was a modified 152mm artillery shell with Russian markings. "It was liberated by one of our agents from Zlatoust-36. You should be able to get confirmation of the loss of this weapon from the Russian government. The fusing and firing system have all been altered to fit our purposes. When it is found, and we have no doubt that you will find it because it is in a well-traveled tourist location, it should not be opened, moved, or tampered with in any way—it will detonate if you do so. Let me repeat: do not open, move, or tamper with that crate! It is our hope that we are not forced to blemish your beautiful city. We will be back in contact with you tomorrow morning to be updated on your progress in meeting our demands and to let you know where to send the fifty million francs."

"Wait. Wait! We need more time. We've talked to the Americans, and they won't release the World Trade Center suspects. The British refuse to consider relinquishing the Rosetta Stone. There's no way we can comply with your demands by Wednesday."

"We're sorry. Inshallah." The line went dead.

Interest turned to alarm. The prime minister was alerted, both to let him know of the problem and to seek his help in figuring out how to handle the thorny matter of asking the Russian government if it had lost one of its nuclear weapons. The mayor of Paris was also briefed. The police did this reluctantly; he had to know, but problems always became louder, more emotional, and more contentious when the mayor became involved. All public order and traffic control police officers, all of the private security forces, and the countless tour guides were instructed to notify the authorities immediately if they saw any containers that looked out of place. The CEA, the French Atomic Energy Commission, was alerted and told to assemble its nuclear counterterrorism team and response equipment and to be prepared to meet in Paris as soon as instructed.

It was not as if this sort of event had not been anticipated. The oft-stated conventional wisdom was that the question was not if nuclear terrorism would occur but when. Over the past decade, this eventuality had received considerable attention from the counterterrorism programs in many countries, particularly the United States, the United Kingdom, and France. Millions of dollars, pounds, and francs had been spent developing technical methods of locating and counteracting different types of nuclear devices. The personnel involved in the various programs had, on occasion, worked together on these developments and knew each other well; everyone now recognized that terrorism was a global rather than national problem.

Almost as soon as the "mysterious box" advisory went out to the various agencies, dozens of reports flooded the temporary command center. The police set up a triage system to investigate the findings; each time a new report arrived, a policeman and a trained detector operator were sent to the site to determine if radioactive material was present. The call from the detection team sent to the Denfert-Rochereau Ossuary in the 14th Arrondissement reported that a suspicious wooden crate in the Catacombs, in the Crypt of the Innocents, emitted a low-level radiation signal. The equipment of the team sent there was not sensitive enough to provide positive identification of the radiation emitter; they would have to wait until a CEA diagnostics team with more sensitive detectors arrived to know for sure. But, with the evidence they had, they were reasonably certain that the box contained some kind of nuclear material, probably plutonium.

The crate was found at 6:00 pm, and by 8:00 pm, when Jean Denis entered the Incident Command Center, the room was full of politicians, police, scientists, and military personnel all demanding information, all insisting on courses of action, all talking at once.

The minister of the interior, officially in charge of terrorism, had appointed the director of public security of the Directorate of the French Police Nationale to be incident commander. Looking around, Jean Denis was able to identify representatives of at least four major agencies surrounding the incident commander: the Parisian prefecture of police, the mayor of Paris, his own CEA, and the French prime minister's office.

By now there were at least fifty people in the Command Center and only twenty-eight seats at the oval incident control table in the middle of the sweltering room. Jean Denis could only shake his head as he noticed that many of the self-important bureaucrats and lower-level military personnel seemed more interested in improving the proximity of their assigned seats to the incident commander's chair than they did in engaging the crisis at hand.

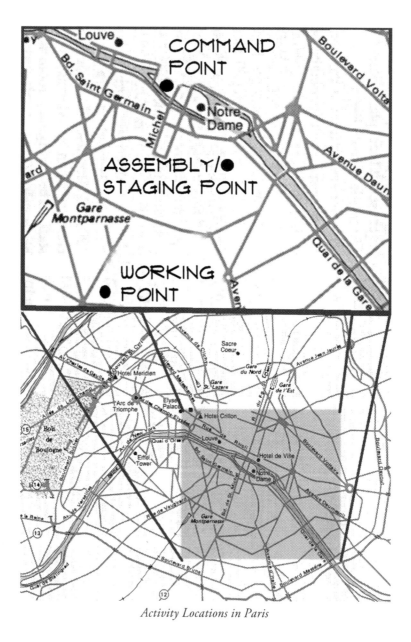

Activity Locations in Paris

Not that he was surprised. After twenty-five years at the CEA, the last five as director of the counterterrorism scientific team, the urbane Jean Denis was no longer surprised by obtuse politicians and military leaders and their scheming functionaries. What did still surprise him was how important so many of them thought they were. To his mind, many of them were bit players in almost any scenario. The resolution of the current situation probably would depend entirely on his team of scientists. The scientists had developed the equipment that would neutralize the weapon, and they would be the ones using that equipment. They had spent their careers preparing for just this type of situation.

Naturally, the military and politicians questioned whether undisciplined, civilian scientists could actually be trusted to show up when the whistle blew. Jean Denis and his team—and their colleagues around the world—did not share this concern; they knew they would be there. On a simplistic level, they wanted to be sure the equipment they had developed was used to its best advantage; on a deeper level, the scientists felt a moral obligation to do what they could if such an event occurred. And, while it probably would never be admitted, there was undoubtedly an element of machismo and adventurism factored into their willingness. They recognized that they might be called upon to risk their lives.

Looking about him, Jean Denis lamented that he had never even set eyes on some of the men now claiming seats around the table; somehow during training exercises, these higher officials had always sent their subordinates, claiming that the pressures of their jobs compelled them to stay in their offices, not lark about in the field. Now they were here to make decisions, even though they had none of the training that would enhance their ability to do so. He smiled grimly as he watched the second-tier decision-makers grab pastries off the refreshment tray and make their way to the incident table; he cynically wondered if any of them would willingly volunteer to be part of his implementation team.

While Jean Denis did not have a seat at the table, his boss did. Jean Denis knew that Giles would effectively represent the CEA's concerns. He was also pleased to recognize the police prevote, a senior police officer who was second in command to the prefect of police. The prevote had regularly participated in their training exercises; Jean Denis knew that he understood the capabilities and needs of the scientific team.

The scientific aspects of the response were not even part of the present discussion. The mayor of Paris had the floor, and he was loudly expounding on what he knew the solution had to be. "There is no decision to be made here folks. Let's stop all this foolish talk of science, detectors, and those goddamned shaped charges. Our only real option is to try to meet the terrorists' demands, and all of our efforts should be directed toward making that happen; the rest of all this is just bullshit. We need to let them know that that's what we're going to do and it's to their advantage to give us some extra time."

His voice level increased with each thought, and his face became an even brighter crimson as he rose to his feet and grabbed at the incident commander's phone. "Give me that damned phone, I'll call whoever it is we need to call to get it all started if you're too intimidated to make the call."

The director of public security angrily moved the mayor's arm away from the phone. "We have never, and I mean never, acceded to a terrorist's extortion demands. That is the acknowledged agreement of the international law enforcement community, and I am certainly not prepared to violate that trust. Have you considered the precedent that would be established? Now please sit down, and let us discuss our options. We most certainly will take your desires into account and act on them should that seem to be the best way out of this mess. Now, please, sir, sit down."

The mayor, obviously reluctant, returned to his seat, still raging. "How about the precedent of destroying cities? Which one of those other countries cares about what happens to Paris? This is bullshit!"

The director glared at him, daring him to speak again. The mayor started to continue his tirade, thought better of it, and resumed his argument in decidedly more hushed tones with an obsequious assistant who was crouching beside him.

"Now," the director continued, obviously angry, "let's see if we can get back to trying to solve this problem rationally. Our embassy in Russia is trying to find out from the Russian authorities if one of their weapons might be missing; we can probably all predict the response to that. The prime minister is talking with the United States to see if they'll release the World Trade Center guys and with the United Kingdom to see if they'll return the Rosetta Stone. Unsurprisingly, both countries' initial reaction was negative." He chuckled ruefully. "What they really said was a variation on 'have you lost your frigging mind?' Even that was more encouraging than our own director of the Louvre. He just laughed when it was suggested that he send the statues of Ramesses and Nakhthorheb back to Egypt.

"But, remember, we're not convinced that the device is real. Please, please, don't start any irreversible actions or take the chance of security leaks until we know for sure. We should have better information within an hour or so. The CEA diagnostic team and an explosive ordnance demolition expert are at the site and we should know more about what's in that box shortly.

"We believe, because so many people have trampled past that box since it was placed in the catacombs sometime yesterday, that no external booby traps, trip wires, or similar devices exist that might cause us to accidentally set off the device as we work around it. The EOD expert's job is to make sure that that is true. After we have determined as well as we can what we have, the EOD will determine if it is possible to gain entry into the box and, if that is so, to safely disable the device. I will let you know when any of this information becomes available from the Working Point.

"In the meantime, we are in the process of setting up a staging/assembly area at the Fifth Arrondissement prefecture on Rue Saint Genevieve—all of the scientific teams and other responders will work from there. Communications between this location and the staging area are already up and running and the necessary communication channels to the Working Point from here and from the staging area are presently being established. Let me repeat once again: any information released to the outside world about this event that comes from anywhere but the Public Information office is forbidden. Such leaks can and will be traced, and I personally promise you that the responsible party will be punished. I do not want to have to send you back to your office, mayor," he said with an impish grin which, to everyone's relief, the mayor returned in reluctant but similar fashion.

"Wait a second," a member of the prime minister's retinue interrupted, "this room and the Fifth Arrondissement prefecture are each less than a kilometer and a half from the device! What if it detonates prematurely? Won't we, along with the guys at the staging area, be wiped out?"

"It's highly unlikely," the director responded. "Our preliminary calculations indicate that we're perfectly safe, even if we have a nuclear detonation."

•　　•　　•

On his way to command the team at the staging area, Jean Denis heard the director's response over his encrypted car radio and shook his head. The actual answer was that, at this point, no one truly knew. The weapons effect team was frantically trying to make meaningful calculations but was finding that the results were highly uncertain. They had to estimate both the yield of the device and the way that the catacombs' spongy limestone would transmit the generated shockwave. The locations of the control point and staging area had been chosen with the assumption that there would be at a safe separation distance, but it certainly was not completely assured.

At the staging area, Jean Denis's mood turned from bad to miserable. Unbelievably, some of the diagnostic equipment used in the last training exercise was missing from its storage locker in Bordeaux, and their sole high-energy imaging device had just been dropped in transit; it was going to require realignment and recalibration. Why, he asked himself, did he have to be a French scientist? His counterparts in the United States and the United Kingdom enjoyed much better government funding and possessed much better equipment, equipment that would be immensely useful in the present situation. He was willing to bet that no one else had to deal with overworked personnel misplacing and dropping equipment. His and the CEA's reputation were at stake, and he had been dealt a miserable hand.

The call from the Working Point brought him out of his gloom and back to the present; the high-sensitivity passive detector was showing a plutonium spectrum emanating from somewhere near the middle of the box. There was no longer any doubt—it was some type of nuclear device. With his call to Giles—"It's certain. We have a nuclear weapon on our hands"—the already frenetic level of activity at command post reached a fevered pitch.

•   •   •

"Okay, okay," the director yelled, attempting to make himself heard over the tumult. "It appears that the threat is real. It's time for a brief discussion from each of you principals telling me what you believe we should do about it, keeping in mind that we have less than four days until the threatened detonation time. Please, let's have ideas, not sermons."

The mayor managed to get his microphone working before anyone else's. "It's entirely obvious. First of all, we need to start evacuation of the city, or at least that part of the Latin Quarter. Then it's essential that we immediately send diplomats, and I mean high-ranking diplomats, to Washington, to London, and to the Louvre to get moving on the release of prisoners and the transfer of the artwork. I can raise the fifty million francs myself if no one else is willing to step up to the table to keep our city from being annihilated. It's ludicrous to be wasting effort discussing any other options; this is not the time to be throwing dice. I agree that all of this will be difficult to do in four days, but I'm sure the terrorists will be willing to extend the deadline if we demonstrate our sincerity in attempting to comply with their demands. But they'll only be willing to do this if we show them that willingness now. If we allow these criminals to—" The mayor continued his fervent plea, but his microphone was cut off as the director interrupted him.

"Yes, mayor, that option will certainly be considered. However, I haven't yet sensed that there is a consensus toward that decision, nor that anyone else agrees with your conclusion. Now what other options do we have?" the director asked, looking at the EOD general de brigade.

"We have two disarmament options. First, we could carefully open the box and sever the connection between the explosive and the firing set. Before we did that, though, we'd need to get good X-rays of the device to make sure that the box was not internally booby-trapped and that the firing set is not in a charged condition. Another option, one which has been used successfully many times in the field, is to identify the location of the firing set by some means and then destroy it with a small explosive, a shaped charge."

"No, no, no, not in my lifetime, never a shaped charge," shouted the mayor, sans microphone, who sat back down after observing the menacing look from the director.

The general, casting an exasperated look in the direction of the interrupting mayor, continued. "This could be disastrous, though, in the unlikely event that the firing set is charged. If it is, we could initiate a full-scale detonation ourselves."

"And you, sir?" the director asked, looking at Giles. "What does the CEA think?"

"We would need more diagnostic information before we attempted disablement, but with that information, we believe we could render the weapon safe with a greatly decreased likelihood of it going nuclear. First, we would take X-rays and gamma ray images of the weapon. Based upon these images, we would then attack the high explosive surrounding the nuclear material with a surgical, high-speed shaped charge, intentionally igniting the explosive but doing it in a manner to minimize the possibility of getting any nuclear yield; that is, we would set off the high explosive in a way that no nuclear event would occur.

"Before firing the shaped charge, we would envelop the weapon with a thick layer of aqueous foam. The foam will rapidly attenuate the shockwave created by the HE detonation, diminishing the ground shock and the damage to the tunnels and adjacent structures. It will also help decrease the size of any crater that might occur, perhaps even making it so that the explosive blast would not be felt outside the catacombs. The second attribute of the foam is that it will capture and contain much of the cloud of radioactive dust that could be generated by the chemical explosion. Without the foam, particulate could be released through the entire tunnel system and on into the atmosphere; costing billions—that's right, billions with a b—of francs to clean up our city.

"For this to work, it is imperative that the weapon not produce a nuclear yield if the high explosive around the plutonium is initiated at a single point; that is, that the weapon must be one-point safe. While they cannot guarantee it, the scientists believe that this is the case and we hope to receive collaborating information from the Russians, assuming that they'll admit that the device is one of their weapons."

The question "one-point what?" came simultaneously from several directions all at once.

"I expected that," Giles continued. "Simply put, in layman's terms, to achieve a nuclear yield, the explosive must compress the nuclear material very uniformly. In early weapons, this was accomplished by igniting the explosive at many points around its periphery; some modern weapons use only two detonators. 'One-point safe' implies that ignition at only one place on the perimeter will not lead to a sufficiently symmetrical compression to produce a nuclear yield. Modern nuclear weapons are all designed to be one-point safe; some very early weapons were not. Chances are good that this device, if it truly is of Russian origin, is one-point safe. If it were of French, UK or US origin, it most certainly would be. Diagnostic data will help us to make that determination, but it would certainly be reassuring to get confirmation from the Russians to corroborate our conclusion.

"Obviously, implementing this solution exposes the people at the Working Point to substantial danger. But we strongly believe it is the surest way to safely dispose of that device.

"There is a final option that I would like to mention before relinquishing the floor," Giles continued, checking with the director to make sure he wasn't exceeding his allotted time. "It is perfectly plausible to do nothing. Almost the only thing we know about this weapon is that it's an old artillery shell, probably Russian. We know that early Russian weapons were not hermetically sealed to prevent exposure of the nuclear materials to the atmosphere. Plutonium corrodes very rapidly. It is quite possible that the plutonium in this weapon is so badly corroded that the weapon will not detonate if we just leave it alone." Finished, Giles sat down, noting the shocked looks on the faces around the table.

"Ignoring the problem is not an option," the director responded forcefully. "There's no way we can do that. How could we justify it to the people of Paris if there were a full-scale nuclear detonation and all we could say is that we didn't think that the bomb would work? That's an option that I suggest we should discard immediately. Does anyone disagree with that?"

No one rose from their seat or raised their hand, so the director continued. "Does anyone else have another plan that we should consider?"

Ignoring the mayor's waving hand, the director continued. "Well then, you've all laid out your suggestions. Let's discuss the advantages and disadvantages of the various options."

The prefect responded immediately. "Capitulating to nuclear blackmail as the mayor suggests would set a precedent that is almost untenable. We believe that needs to be considered only as a last resort. I believe that before we even consider it, we should give the International Association of Police Chiefs a chance to voice their position."

This latest comment was met by derision by one of the mayor's staff. "Paris is our Paris. We don't need any international organization telling us how to protect our city!"

"I do not believe it's necessary to make any decision right now. I see no problem for now in continuing to pursue all options until we get more information," the general de brigade suggested.

"What could we possibly find out that would change anyone's mind?" the mayor challenged. "There's only one realistic solution and you're unwilling to consider it."

"Well, first," the general responded, his face reddening and voice rising, "the explosives detonation team needs more information. We need to know if we could trigger anything if we opened the box. We need to know if the terrorists can communicate with the device and arm it if they detect that we're attempting a render-safe procedure. We need to know the type of power supply that's in use—will the weapon function if we attempt to destroy the firing system? Of course, it would really help if we had good images of the device. Finally, we need to have some confidence that the device is one-point safe if we intentionally initiate the explosive system. God, I wish we could find out who built that bloody thing and exactly what it is!" With that, the general slapped his notebook down on the table in front of him, quite obviously frustrated at having to reiterate the obvious problems to someone unwilling to listen.

Predictably, the mayor rose to his feet, shouting "I don't—"

"Thank you," the director responded. "Anyone else?" No response.

"Okay. Now we need to consider evacuation plans. I've already met with the prefect, and if evacuation becomes necessary, we'll announce on Tuesday morning that there's been a massive chlorine spill near the intersection of Rue Remy Dumoncel and Rue d' Alambert. We'll stage a truck collision and release a small amount of chlorine to substantiate the cover story. We will then alert the four hospitals within five hundred meters of the Working Point, letting them know that we may need to evacuate their patients.

"We've already taken precautions to prevent information leaks. The security in this building is at its highest possible level. You've all signed affidavits not to disclose the incident, we've confiscated your personal cell phones, and, unless you have permission to leave, you are all expected to stay within the building for the duration. Your families will be told that you are participating in a surprise nationwide antiterrorism exercise and that they can contact you only through the monitored phone system set up in the adjacent room. I'm sure all these precautions won't keep the incident completely secret, but they should go a long way toward preventing a fiasco.

"We're currently attempting to secure the Working Point as much as possible. As you can image, sealing off the catacombs is a massive headache— we can barricade the public entrances, but there are almost countless uncharted ways into and out of those tunnels. I'm confident we're doing the best we can there, but anyone who emerges unexpectedly from one of the tunnels will be held by the police for the duration of the incident."

Sighing heavily, the director continued. "Unfortunately, we can't guarantee the success of anything we're doing here. But, I think we're headed in the right direction. Our next step depends greatly on the information we're able to gather in the next twenty-four hours."

• • •

Listening to the director on the police radio network, Jean Denis glumly surveyed the police station warehouse that was serving as the staging area and assembly point: people and equipment performing a seemingly haphazard dance that had only now started to assume some semblance of order. His CEA scientific team members were on their way to Paris from all over the country; he'd be extremely relieved when they arrived with whatever working equipment they had been able to assemble.

But, he thought, I don't hold much hope for our success. Our equipment isn't good enough for this emergency. I wish we had the American equipment. Hell, I wish we had the Americans, too. They're not any smarter than us, but they'd be a great sounding board. I would love to be able to talk this over with Bise.

When his team finally arrived, they were subdued. Instead of their usual friendly banter, the conversation centered on where the missing equipment was and what to do about the damaged high-energy imaging device. Jean Denis's alternate team leader, Pierre, offered the seemingly offhand idea that maybe they could borrow some equipment from the Americans. The rest of the discouraged group quickly embraced this concept, conjecturing what they might be able to accomplish with this more-sophisticated equipment.

"But," Pierre interjected, "we really aren't familiar with how their stuff works. Maybe we need to borrow their scientists too." The rest of the team jumped on this suggestion, and Jean Denis smiled at Pierre. It wasn't the first time Pierre had given voice to Jean Denis's personal thoughts. *God bless my chubby friend*, Jean Denis thought.

Jean Denis was afraid that the damnable French pride would get in the way of their proposal and that the French authorities would be reluctant to ask anyone for assistance. Sometimes there's no room for pretensions, he thought. We need help and it's ridiculous to let national egos stand in the way. He knew, and admired, the members of the American team, and he suspected they would be only too willing to help.

This is exactly what he found himself telling Giles on the phone: "I'd really like a few of their scientists and their rapid response package. I believe that it's almost certain that they'd be willing to come, Giles. We wouldn't expect them to participate at the Working Point, but they know how their equipment works and we don't. Does this make sense to you? Would you and the prefect be willing to discuss it with the director?"

"It's a great idea, Jean Denis. I wish I had thought of it. Let me talk to the prefect and see if I can convince him. If he's game, then we'll go to the director. It may be a hard sell to the bureaucrats—we're essentially admitting that the Americans are more prepared and better equipped than we are.

Personally, I think you're right—this isn't a time for French pride. I'll go right now and see if I can corner the prefect, and I'll let you know how we're progressing."

After a quick consultation, Giles and the prefect approached the director. He was surprisingly receptive to the suggestion, and within minutes they were meeting with a representative from the prime minister's office who promised to call the French embassy in Washington immediately and ask the ambassador to start the process.

Seizing an opportunity to enhance the diplomatic relationship with France, the US Embassy responded quickly. They would be pleased to assist, contingent upon approval from the Department of Energy, the US agency that owned the equipment and, of course, the scientists.

Admiral Grangly, the head of the Department of Energy's Nuclear Weapon Programs, saw no downside to the proposal: in fact, he saw several strong reasons to agree. First, it would help justify the decade of expenditures involved in developing the response program; maybe he would no longer have to hear, as he did during every single congressional budget cycle, "We're tired of sinking all of this money on your scientific hobby shop and training. When has this response team and their fancy equipment ever been used?" Secondly, the French assured him that the risk to the American scientists would be minimal because they would be operating in an advisory capacity only. The third reason was admittedly somewhat selfish and embarrassing: his participating in the Paris crisis would be a hell of a lot more interesting than the quarterly program review that was presently on the agenda for the coming week.

The United States was ready, willing, and able to come to France's assistance. Perhaps they were even anxious.

CHAPTER TWO
Bison
Sunday, September 10, 1995

Bison was languorously mowing his much-loved bluegrass lawn when he heard the phone ring. He knew that the call was important when Bev came out of the house in her slippers to get him; she had been giving him the silent treatment all morning because she was still upset about last night.

I guess I'll never learn, he thought as he remembered the evening. Bev's Saturday night bridge group had met at their house. Exiled to his study, the mischievous Bison had had plenty of time to devise some entertainment for these women who, this evening, seemed unusually quiet and humorless.

He filled an empty wastebasket with water and, leaving the door to the bedroom open, proceeded to very slowly empty the wastebasket into the toilet from shoulder height; the emptying process, he estimated, must have taken a full five minutes. He could hear a few sniffles of suppressed embarrassed laughter when he was about halfway through, the laughter gradually increasing until he was finally finished. He then swaggered down the hall, smiled broadly at the women gathered around the card tables in the living room, and proceeded to the kitchen, where he retrieved a beer from the refrigerator and opened it loudly. He was sure every member of his audience except Beverly had wanted to applaud, but in deference to their hostess, had refrained. From the corner of his eye, he noted that his dear bride was giving him that familiar "wait until later" glare.

Now here she was, out on the lawn in the middle of the day, questioning and concerned. "Admiral Grangly wants you to call him. It sounds really important."

Bise knew it had to be important; the DC-based head of the Department of Energy's Department of Military Application did not make frivolous Sunday phone calls.

When Bison returned the call, the normally jovial admiral was extremely serious. "Are you on a secure phone?"

"No, I'm at home. Give me twenty-five minutes and I'll call you back."

Bison gave Bev a quick kiss on his way out the door. "I have no idea what's going on. I'll let you know if I'm going to be longer than an hour."

On his drive to the lab, Bison tried to guess what the admiral wanted. Apparently there was a potentially viable nuclear threat somewhere in the world. Most likely it was not in the United States; if it had been, Admiral Grangly would have been orchestrating the response, not personally making phone calls. So it was a problem someplace else. Why had he been called? Did the problem require some unusual expertise that only he and his team possessed? As the result of their periodic multinational antiterrorism exercises, the participants always acknowledged that they would try and make themselves available to assist each other no matter where on the globe the problem occurred; terrorism really had no national boundaries. The scientists knew that their program administrators were in favor of this type of cooperation: not only did it give the various organizations the opportunity to assist in dealing with whatever current problem existed, it also was a strong bargaining chip in the never-ending discussion of funding allocations.

When Bison placed the secure call from the lab, the admiral himself answered the phone. "The French believe that a rogue nuclear device is hidden in Paris; the supposed detonation time is Wednesday at 1700 hours. They've asked for our help. It sounds like they are more interested in our equipment than in our personnel; they keep stressing that we're to act only as advisors and that we're not responsible for any of the Working Point activities. Will you lead the US team? If so, I promise you complete autonomy in choosing who you want to take with you. If you can go, get in touch with the Las Vegas DOE office, and be prepared to leave for France from Nellis Air Force Base tomorrow at 0900 hours on a Dassault Falcon 900 that the French are sending."

There was a long silence. Impatiently, the admiral pressed, "Bison, will you do this for me?"

"Sir, I want to. I need to check on some personal obligations. Let me see what I can work out, and I'll call you back within the hour." Bison had some decidedly mixed emotions as he hung up the phone. He wanted to go to Paris because it was the perfect opportunity for his team to gain real experience: actual, time-constrained experience, not the hokey, contrived situations of training events. He also knew that agreeing to go could bring economic favor upon his program. But he was suspicious of why he had been the one they called. He was pretty certain he was not headquarters' favorite of the various possible team leaders.

The timing could not be worse. His only daughter, "Princess" to all who knew her, was getting married the coming Friday evening, forty-eight short hours after the alleged detonation time. The wedding was going to be a massive event, several acquaintances and relatives flying in from overseas. *It's probably going to cost me more than this terrorist event is going to cost the French government,* he thought ruefully. There was no way he was going to miss the wedding.

He called Bev, explaining the situation without compromising security. Predictably, she was less than pleased. "Are you seriously considering missing your only daughter's wedding? She'd be devastated! And," she continued, displaying the humorously sardonic side he had loved all these years, "you know how long you've waited to give her away."

"I know. Believe me, that's my top consideration. I'll be home for the wedding. They've promised me that no matter what I'll be home on Thursday evening even if they have to fly me back on one of their military planes," he lied. No such discussion had taken place, but the scenario was certainly possible. They talked for a few more minutes, Bev gradually becoming more receptive to the idea, and then Bison said "I won't be home for dinner tonight, but I'll stop to pick up some clothes before I leave for Vegas. I think that this will all work out, Bev, I really do. I love you."

"Princess and I certainly hope so," she replied.

As he hung up the phone, he realized why he had been chosen to lead the US delegation: Jean Denis. Collaborating over the years, he and his French colleague had become extremely close friends. He was certain that Jean Denis had asked for him by name, knowing that Bison would not hesitate to help and that the two scientists could work well together.

Bison dialed the admiral, who was much happier with his decision than Bev had been. "I think I've got it all figured out, sir. I do need your assurance on a couple of matters. My daughter is getting married on Friday night. I need to be home by Thursday afternoon, even if it involves chartering an aircraft. That's the first condition, and I'm afraid that it has to be unconditional. The second is that, given the stakes and the time constraints, I need autonomy. I need the authority to choose the appropriate people, to control who and what goes on the aircraft, and to make those decisions without a lot of discussion and outside interference. Do you think this is doable?"

"Of course," the admiral assured him. "You have my word on both counts."

"Thank you, sir. If more information comes through or if you need to get in touch with me, I will be here at my office for a few hours trying to assemble a team and make the logistical arrangements. I'll give you a call when I leave."

"That sounds reasonable. For your information, I have asked the French to land their plane at Andrews Air Force Base on the way back since they have to refuel anyway. I'll meet you there. I'll have some of my staff with me, and I'm sure some of the Las Vegas people will also want to go to Paris. We'll probably have a real planeload. But the important thing is to get your team and your equipment over there as fast as possible. If there's no room for us, we can always follow commercially."

"Thank you, sir," Bison replied, while muttering to the empty office, "I thought I had control of the aircraft."

His next call was to Jean Denis to find out just what was going on. He needed a lot more information before he boarded the plane: did he need to bring search equipment, or had they already found the device? What kind of device did they think it was? In addition, he wanted to hear his friend's voice and assure him they were on the way.

It took an hour, but Bison finally found Jean Denis. "I hear you need my help. Again," Bison joked, knowing that Jean Denis would recognize the reference to a long-ago incident in Las Vegas involving the police and a speeding Corvette.

He winced at the strain and fatigue in his friend's voice. "I apologize, Bise, for getting you involved in this. Our equipment is in shambles and there's no way we can handle it alone. I'm convinced that the threat is real. We've found the device. It is in one of the caverns in the catacombs, not far from Notre Dame and the Louvre. We've already been down to the chamber and have taken a few detector readings. We are convinced that it's an old Russian 152mm shell that's probably been rewired. We also suspect that they've built in some devices to prevent tampering. All the principle politicians are presently mingling in our War Room; the shouting and arm waving have already started. You're the best news that has happened since all of this started, and I can't express my gratitude enough for your coming. I promise to get you home in time for Princess's big day."

Bison smiled at his friend's characteristic sensitivity; he had forgotten that Jean Denis and Christine were invited to the wedding. The two men exchanged information to ensure that the avenues of communication would remain open and then hung up.

Bison's phone rang immediately. It was PJ, a supernumerary (or as Bison's boss called them, straphangers) from the Department of Energy field office in Nevada. The DOE had been alerted to the pending operation by headquarters and they had "just a few" suggestions regarding team composition and logistics. They also wanted to be sure that Bison saved at least three seats on the plane for the Nevada contingent. "You need to remember, Bison," PJ continued, "there is a difference between laboratory and federal employees and who is authorized to do what."

Bison had never understood the amorphous boundary separating watchers from doers, but he knew he was on one side and PJ was on the other. "PJ, I will keep that under consideration, and I imagine that there are going to be several headquarters people who also want a ride. The admiral has assured me that I have the authority to pick the team and that those team members and their equipment have first priority for space on the plane. I do need you to get all of the rapid-response equipment on the pad at Nellis by 8:00 am tomorrow morning along with a loading crew and load-master. Can you do that?"

"Everything will be ready for you. Just don't forget those seats."

"Can't promise a thing, but I've got three Nevada seats on my 'if there's room' list. Now I need to get off the phone so I can assemble my team."

"That sounds good, Bise, we'll look forward to seeing you tomorrow morning. Between us, I think we can really help the French on this."

As PJ hung up, Bison realized that the seating situation was going to become an enormous problem, but it was one he didn't have to deal with until everyone who wanted a seat was on the tarmac at Nellis tomorrow. He had more urgent things to worry about now.

Bison began to build a team in his mind. He needed two effects people to calculate the consequences of a nuclear or other explosive detonation; two weapon physicists to decipher the internal composition of the device from the diagnostic data; two engineers to devise the disablement scheme; and, finally, two people to guide the erection of a containment structure if that proved to be included in the solution. With him, that made a total of nine plus all of their equipment, an easy fit on the Dassault 900. There should even be a few seats left over.

He then considered who he would like to have fill each of these positions and began making his recruitment phone calls. To his amazement, he was able to run down each of his choices by 7:00 pm. Even more startling, each of them was able to comprehend his rather cryptic request without having to take the time to find a secure phone line. With one exception, they were all able and willing to participate. Almost everyone he talked to offered quite a bit of advice about team composition; he soon realized that he had to get away from his phone as soon as possible because he was going to start receiving calls from other potential team members he had not picked to go.

Bison sensed that each of the men was flattered to be chosen. They had all made it clear that he would owe them—the term "big time" was used more than once—but he knew that they all appreciated the confidence he had in them. He also knew that he was going to have to smooth the ruffled feathers of some of the potential candidates he had not chosen. Oh, the glory of leadership, he thought. I wanted to be an engineer, not a manager.

He then called Admiral Grangly, leaving a message that he could be reached at home for the next hour and then would be flying to Las Vegas. "If everything goes well, we'll see you out at Andrews tomorrow afternoon."

• • •

Early the next morning, Bison looked around the tarmac at Nellis Air Base just outside Las Vegas. Here was a group of men about to depart for one of the world's most sophisticated cities, and it looked like he had raided the homeless shelter. He knew he had chosen the right men for the situation. He knew their capabilities, and he enjoyed their often-ribald personalities. Even though some had not seen each other in months, the teasing had begun. He was proud of his scruffy warriors. *But geez,* he thought, *couldn't they have put a little more energy into dressing respectfully?*

Then he caught a glimpse of himself reflected by the early morning sun on the aircraft fuselage. The snaps on his bright orange windbreaker could not quite contain his expanding paunch, and he probably could have chosen better than the soiled Pabst Blue Ribbon baseball cap. A nearly white three-day beard completed the elegant ensemble. "Yep," Bison reflected, smiling at his earlier superiority, "I'm with them."

A four-man Nevada DOE contingent, to a man nattily dressed in pressed slacks and shirts and bolo ties, waited off to the side while Bison and the field office director discussed how much extra room there was on the French Dassault. The director was very solicitous and agreed with Bison that the first priority was the scientists and their equipment. They concluded that there was room for the director and one other field officer, and the remaining field officers would follow on a commercial flight.

As the director approached his men, Bison could hear PJ loudly pleading his case. Bison saw the director shake his head, and within minutes the lab scientists, the director, and his assistant were on board, leaving PJ and his well-traveled briefcase standing discontentedly on the tarmac.

After a brief stop at Andrews Air Force Base to refuel and pick up Admiral Grangly, the Dassault was on its way across the Atlantic to Paris. Within fifteen minutes, all the interior lights were either off or dimmed; this was possibly the last sleep anyone on board would get until the situation in Paris was resolved. Bison tried to stay awake to review his game plan; it was a losing battle.

He was still dozing when the director's assistant from Nevada tapped his arm. "Bise, Admiral Grangly wants to talk to you."

The admiral had been on the phone with the command center in Paris.

"I've been talking to the police prefect. There's no new technical information, but they do have some poor quality X-rays and part of it certainly looks like a nuclear artillery shell. There are some major components attached to the front of the shell that they don't recognize, though. The usual political bullshit is happening: the mayor wants nothing to do with what he calls 'this scientific madness' and is ready to give into the terrorists' demands; the police prefect says there's no way he's going to capitulate to terrorism. Fortunately we don't have to deal with the mayor.

"We'll land about 9:00 am; you and your team will be taken directly to the assembly point, which is at a police academy less than a mile from their Ground Zero. Jean Denis will meet you and give you an up-to-date technical briefing. Everyone whose presence is not immediately required should try and get some rest after the briefing; the facility has beds, showers, and food. No rest for you, though. Jean Denis wants you and your diagnosticians to help him determine an action plan. He also would like your effects people to meet up with his guys and start calculating immediately; they've made some preliminary estimates but Jean Denis thinks those estimates are far too conservative. The rest of the DOE guys and I will be at the control point. There will be a direct phone line between you and me, and we need to keep in communication.

"I think that's it, Bise, now go get some sleep. You're going to need it. And, Bise," the admiral continued, putting his hand on Bise's shoulder, "thanks so much for coming. You know I have the utmost confidence in you."

Glad you do, Bise thought as he made his way back to his seat, because right now that makes one of us.

CHAPTER THREE
Jean Denis
Monday, September 11, 1995

The noise level in the command center on the Isle de Cite was a constant rumble. Trying to reach consensus on how to deal with the problem seemed impossible. Each faction had its favorite course of action, and no one seemed interested in even considering anyone else's point of view. Should the city be evacuated? If so, when? Was there any hope that further conversations with the terrorists would produce any useful information? Would—and could— the terrorists extend the deadline? Which render-safe procedure would be the most appropriate? Would it be possible to disable the device without initiating a nuclear detonation?

Almost everyone at command center agreed that a wholesale evacuation of the city was out of the question. The mayor had initially protested that his first duty was to protect his citizenry, so of course the city should be evacuated; when it was pointed out that he would always be closely linked with the hysteria and fear accompanying such an evacuation, he realized that this could cloud his political future forever and the issue of full-scale evacuation disappeared.

Under the cover story that yet another serious fault in the hospital's ancient heating and cooling system had been discovered—and that the total failure of the system was imminent—the eighty elderly patients at the La Rochefoucald Hospital had been moved to a facility well outside the range of the bomb's effects. The public uproar surrounding yet another hospital evacuation was so severe that the politicians decided not to evacuate the other hospitals in the vicinity until it was critically necessary.

In the quiet of a small conference room next to the Control Room, the prevote needed answers about the scientific response to the emergency. Searching Giles's and Jean Denis's faces, he asked, "Just how bad is it going to be? What can we expect and what decisions are we going to have to make?"

Jean Denis was somber. "I can't put good numbers on things yet, but I can describe what we can expect if a nuclear detonation occurs. First, the device is essentially buried in limestone and gypsum, which will absorb the initial radiation burst; that's very helpful. Upon detonation, the material directly over the device will be propelled upward and, depending upon the nuclear yield, will either fall right back into the cavity the blast has produced or—more probably—the yield will be large enough to throw all the debris outward, forming a crater at least ten meters in radius with a six- to eight-meter lip. A radioactive cloud will probably escape from the cavern and cover much of the city. We can't be more specific until we have better estimates on the yield of the device and how the limestone and gypsum will respond to the shock from the detonation."

"So"—the prevote struggled to understand the science—"if the material over the device falls back into the cavity, it will seal itself off, and all we have to worry about is the dust that is kind of 'burped' up? There won't be any other damage?"

"Unfortunately that's not the case," Jean Denis answered. "The detonation will generate a strong ground and air shock that can destroy buildings within hundreds of meters. Then, a high-pressure gaseous cloud containing fission fragments will spread through the catacombs, and if the cavity isn't sealed completely, out into the city."

"I'm really frustrated. You're still talking in generalities and not giving me anything to work with! What's the radius of damage for the destroyed buildings? How am I supposed to plan evacuations and other precautions if I don't know how much damage there will be? I need to figure out how to save lives!"

"I'm sorry, sir," Jean Denis replied, "but this is the best I can do right now. I really can't be more specific."

"Will it be meters, kilometers, what?" the prevote persisted. "Will the destruction extend up to the Seine; are the Metro tunnels and the sewer system in danger? Can't we figure this out on our own? Don't we have any capability? Or do we always have to wait for the Americans to swoop in and save the day?"

Jean Denis and Giles exchanged a glance, and Giles nodded. "Well," Jean Denis said to the prevote, "I understand your frustration. We do have some cursory estimates, but I was reluctant to share them with you because I don't have a great deal of faith in their accuracy, and they might change by as much as a factor of two or three. The uncertainty is not so much in the analytical method as it is in the input conditions like the weapon yield and the dynamic response of the walls of the chamber. We do anticipate getting a better fix on these values shortly. But here's what we have right now."

Pulling a folded piece of paper from his pocket, he continued. "First, we're pretty certain we're dealing with a Russian 152mm fission plutonium implosion device. The maximum yield obtainable in a pristine, modern device of this type is probably one hundred tons HE equivalent, and we've used that estimate in our calculations; we'd expect that the yield of this older, probably corroded weapon to be significantly less, perhaps by as much as half. With the one-hundred-ton yield, we'd anticipate that the overhead surface would be breached, that a crater of about a ten-meter radius would be left, and that tall buildings out to perhaps one hundred fifty meters would be in danger; this would include the area from just south of La Rochefoucald to Rue Bezout and from where Rue Halle bends south in the west, to just across the Metro tracks in the east. We also expect that a significant cloud of radioactive material and pulverized overburden will be released to the atmosphere. This will require inhabitants downwind to stay indoors for a period of time and be forced to wear breathing protection if they must go outside. It will also result in a cost of billions of francs and months or even years to completely clean up the radioactive fallout. We do not believe the Seine casings are in any danger or that any Metro or sewer tunnels will be threatened."

The prevote sat quietly for a long moment. "Mon dieu! That's a terrible prediction, but I guess I honestly thought it could be much worse. When will you have better numbers? I'm particularly concerned about building damage and evacuation, since that's the only thing we seem to be able to do much about."

"We'll have more information later this evening. We'll also have more confidence in the predictions when the Americans get here tomorrow. They'll have different dynamic response models for the gypsum and limestone and a different method of making these calculations—we'll need to compare our results with theirs. Also, the numbers are very sensitive to the device yield, and the area involved would be decreased by more than half if the expected yield turns out to be, say, ten tons."

"Okay, I understand the difficulty, but let me know immediately when you have figures you trust more. Even if Giles needs to pull me out of a meeting," the prevote said as he rose, indicating to Giles and Jean Denis that their audience was over.

As they prepared to leave—Giles to return to his assigned seat in the control center and Jean Denis to the assembly area—the prevote called them back. "One more thing. What can we expect will happen if we use some of this scientific magic you guys are always bragging about?"

For the first time in hours, Giles smiled. "I'm pleased that you thought to ask that, we should have brought it up ourselves. Jean Denis, have you made any of those predictions?"

"That's a completely different story—I suspect that you will consider it to be good news. Do you want the one-minute or ten-minute version?"

"Let's have the whole story. I'll need to know it sometime and it will postpone my going back out there to be berated by the mayor again."

"Okay. There are several options we can pursue; the risk of each depends upon the amount of information that we possess. The quickest and simplest is an attack on the firing system, either in a hands-on operation or with a small shaped charge. If we try this and it works, the game is over; there will be neither a nuclear detonation nor a detonation of the weapon explosive, there will be no cleanup, and we'll all be heroes. However, it is the riskiest operation and if it fails, we will quite possibly trigger a full-scale nuclear detonation, complete with all of the consequences we've just described.

"A less risky procedure would be to intentionally initiate the high explosive surrounding the nuclear core at a single point. This works only if we are confident that initiation at this location would result in such a highly asymmetrical compression of the nuclear core that little or no nuclear yield results. All French, British, and US weapons currently stockpiled are designed so that this type of initiation will not result in a nuclear detonation. We assume that modern Russian weapons share this characteristic, but we're not sure. The Embassy is currently trying to get this information from the Russians. If we can get good diagnostic pictures of the device, we may be able to get this assurance for ourselves, based upon our design experience and previous testing that has been done on similar devices. These images will also help us decide where it's best to attack the device with a shaped charge should we decide on this course of action. Are you still with me?"

"Yes, but don't we still have a problem if we just set off the high explosives?"

"Yes we do, but we're talking the difference of about ten thousand times in the amount of energy released—about fifteen kilos of high explosive yield and one hundred tons nuclear. While detonation of this amount of HE may cause a bit of a mess in the Innocents cavern, a much more significant problem is that some thirty grams or so of the weapon's plutonium may be aerosolized."

"But don't I remember from previous exercises that you can cover the device with runway foam and capture most of that material? Is it not possible to do that?"

"You're absolutely right. If there is sufficient space and if time permits, we'll erect a containment structure and then, near detonation time, fill it with dense aqueous foam. As you probably also remember, this foam does two things for us. Assuming that there's no nuclear event, it will almost completely contain the blast wave within the cavern. And, just as importantly, the foam will capture practically all of the aerosol-sized particulate generated by the HE detonation. While we'll be left with a gunky, foamy mess in the immediate area in the cavern, the aerosol contamination to the city will essentially be eliminated."

"But how do we decide which of the several options to choose?" The prevote was beginning to understand the magnitude of the decision he was going to have to make.

Jean Denis smiled inwardly at the prevote's perception before he answered. "We will keep you informed through Giles as we go along. While we may offer our advice, the ultimate decision, of course, is yours and the prefect's. Undoubtedly you will be getting input and advice from at least a dozen other sources; I'd guess the mayor will help."

"I'm not so sure how much authority we and the mayor will actually have," the prevote replied. "We just heard that the prime minister will join us in the morning, and if he shows, it probably will become his call."

This was dismaying news to Jean Denis. The more high-level bureaucrats involved, the more politically driven the decision was likely to become.

"There is one other factor in all of this that you should be aware of," Giles injected. "To get the information we need in order to employ these more sophisticated solutions, there will be as many as six people working for an extended period in the proximity of a weapon which could, either intentionally or inadvertently, detonate at any time. This is frightening to me. We need to assure these people that, whatever course of action is chosen, their welfare will always be our foremost consideration."

"You have my word on that," responded the prevote, beginning to rise from his chair, indicating either that he'd had as much of this scientific discussion as he could handle at the moment or that he felt it was time to get back to the inevitable, unpleasant discussions with the mayor.

Jean Denis, however, was not quite ready to relinquish the prevote's attention. "While we've got you here, we'd like to get your approval to send the Explosive Ordnance Demolition team down to the Working Point to try and get some additional information about the device—the sooner the better."

The prevote frowned. "I can't give you that approval, but let's see if we can get a few minutes of the prefect's attention. Can you two stick around for a few minutes while I see what I can set up?"

"Of course," Giles and Jean Denis replied in near unison.

•   •   •

While Giles returned to his assigned seat at the Control table, Jean Denis took the opportunity to eavesdrop on the discussions taking place in different corners of the room. The evacuation of La Rochefoucald was progressing more rapidly than had been expected. Beds in other hospitals were being located in case it became necessary to begin evacuating Sainte-Anne's tomorrow. The plans for the staged truck accident and the chlorine release were all set for the next day, which was Tuesday Jean Denis had to remind himself, since he was beginning to lose track of time. The police were prepared to cordon off an area bounded by General LeClerc, Saint Jacques, Rue Dareau, Rue Broussais, and Rue d' Alesia after the chlorine was released. Everyone in that area would be required to leave for at least two nights and public transportation and accommodations would be provided for those who needed it; no private vehicles would be permitted to enter the cordoned area. It was estimated that the area could be cleared and people who had no place else to go could all be moved to the temporary shelters within twenty-four hours. "They're kidding themselves about that," Jean Denis mumbled to himself. But, he didn't have enough evidence to argue that point, and it really wasn't within his purview so he moved to the opposite side of the room to remove his temptation to intercede.

Here the debate about how best to deal with the terrorists was raging loudly and vehemently. The American government was apparently willing— quite reluctantly—to turn the World Trade Center perpetrators over to the French government; the mayor's office itself was prepared to come up with the money the terrorists had demanded. Although he knew the final decision rested with the prime minister, the director of the Louvre was objecting adamantly to the removal of the two colossals, citing, among other things, the absolute ridiculousness of attempting to safely move such treasures within a two-day time period. The British were similarly recalcitrant; they didn't believe that a country should ever allow itself to be blackmailed by terrorists and, to them, the possibility of giving up prized possessions to accede to terrorist demands was viewed as yet another example of the famed French timidity.

And so the argument in the Control Point raged. Jean Denis could not discover when or how the next contact with the terrorists was going to take place, but he was glad he was not the police terrorist negotiator who was going to have to make sense out of the entire accumulation of contradictory clamor. He also realized that the chance of getting additional technical information about the device during future calls from the terrorists was virtually nil; they would have to rely on whatever the Russians themselves might offer and what his scientific team might be able to generate.

He was helping himself to a sandwich from the sumptuous buffet—featuring much more expensive wine than he drank at home—when Giles appeared at his side. "We're set to meet with the prefect and prevote right after the 6:00 pm briefing, which should start in just a few minutes."

Although he was anxious to get the EOD process underway, Jean Denis was interested in hearing firsthand where the various individuals felt the process stood. Grabbing another sandwich, he wedged himself into a corner to listen.

The briefing was a disappointment. Jean Denis did not learn anything new as each of the organizations involved in the decision-making presented a three-minute status update. The mayor, predictably, spent much longer than three minutes elucidating his concerns, and several of the bureaucratic players spent their time outlining their many qualifications rather than presenting any solutions or updates. *"Do these jokers really think they're as important as they're pretending to be?"* Jean Denis wondered, not for the first time in his career.

Shortly after 7:00 pm, he and Giles were summoned into the prefect's private chamber, a conference room with six chairs, a couch, a cot, and a bathroom. "I understand we need to talk about activities at the Working Point," the prefect began.

With a nod, Giles deferred to Jean Denis. "We're ready to start the EOD work but felt we should not do so without your permission. How much detail would you like?"

"Very little, I guess. I don't know enough about the science part of it to make an informed decision. I either have to trust your judgment or not. If I didn't, you wouldn't be standing here. So go ahead and start your work. Giles, will keep me apprised of your progress? I would like to discuss your plans in detail before you begin the disablement phase, but until then, continue on; I don't want to hold you up. Giles, I assume you will be here should I have any questions?"

Giles nodded, and he and Jean Denis turned to leave. "I believe, gentlemen," the prefect concluded, "that the ultimate solution to this problem will be in your hands. And I truly believe that the French government will never accede to the demands of terrorists, no matter how loud the mayor yells."

• • •

Lack of sleep finally caught up with Jean Denis on the short ride back to the assembly area. Dozing off, he fantasized that the Americans had already arrived and were in the catacombs, all set up, impatiently waiting for his permission to begin the diagnostics. Bolting awake as the police transport came to a stop, he realized he had been dreaming—it was still early Tuesday morning and his overseas cohorts would not arrive for nearly six hours. While awaiting their arrival, he needed to see what progress was possible with the meager resources they had at hand.

Stepping into the conference room just off the gymnasium-like area where the available equipment was being unpacked and calibrated, Jean Denis spotted the EOD commander and his lieutenant. He had tremendous respect for these grizzled, serious veterans of bomb disposal; other members of the response team might have greater technical expertise and understanding, but none had proven their capability in the field nearly as often as the EOD operatives.

Their expertise and zeal, though, could be both an attribute and a weakness. They had no patience for the often long, drawn-out decision-making that the scientists preferred—they wanted action, and they wanted to do it now. Their preferred form of action with an explosive device was to disable it by cutting the electrical leads with a pair of wire cutters or blowing it apart with a shaped charge. Neither approach was necessarily appropriate when dealing with a rogue nuclear device; the negative consequences of such actions could be disastrous.

"We're all briefed and ready to go," the commander replied. "We've gone over our plan with Pierre and he approves. Do we have the okay from up top to proceed?"

"Yes, but let's review what you believe you have the approval to do, and what you don't have the approval to do. We need to be completely clear on this."

The commander bristled; he didn't like the delay, and he didn't like being challenged by a scientist who admittedly did not have a lot of field experience. "I certainly hope our approach meets with your approval. We're going to use the laser tool and drill a five-millimeter hole in the upper-left-hand corner of the box. This is a slow process, but we're afraid that the vibration of an ordinary drill might set off the device. When we have a hole, we'll insert our observational scope to see if we can identify a firing set and determine where the detonator cables are running. We'll also be able to determine if there are wires running to the firing system, which might indicate a protective membrane. Then we'll drill another 5mm hole near the upper right rear corner of the box to give us a view of the interior from the opposite perspective.

"The view from the two holes may give us an idea of how to disable the device. If we see a solution in which we have a high degree of confidence, we'd like to get the okay to go ahead with the action with a minimum of debate. The longer a decision takes, the more dangerous the situation becomes."

"I appreciate your position, and I agree with it, but I don't see much chance of a rapid decision. The way the politicians are carrying on we'll be lucky to have a decision by zero time. But you will have my complete support, and I promise to do what I can to expedite things."

"Good enough, that's all I can ask. We'll keep you posted."

"Thank you, good luck, and God bless." Jean Denis felt a surge of adrenaline as he watched the first of his team leave to join the menacing situation in the Cemetery of the Innocents.

Next, he yelled for Pierre to come give him a status report. Pierre, who had been down at the far end of the cavernous gymnasium talking to one of the female effects calculators, ran up to Jean Denis, gasping for breath. "Damned cigarettes," Pierre puffed, oblivious to the fifteen extra kilograms around his waist.

"Right," Jean Denis said as he smiled, "blame the cigarettes. What's going on?"

Pierre reported that the efforts of the effects, containment, and disablement teams were all proceeding relatively smoothly, but that the diagnostic team was hamstrung by its faulty equipment. "We can get some low energy X-ray pictures, but they're going to be next to useless. We're really out of luck until Bise and his team get here," Pierre concluded. "Really smart of you, Boss, to suggest that we call the Americans over."

Chuckling because he knew that both he and Pierre knew it had been Pierre's idea to enlist the Americans, Jean Denis checked in with Giles at the command center. Giles quickly ran down all the pertinent developments; the fake chlorine spill had occurred and the evacuation of the area around the Catacombs was proceeding without incident; so far the media was not spreading any rumors about a nuclear device; meeting the ransom demands looked impossible, and it was becoming apparent that a political solution would only happen with the participation of presidents and prime ministers, a solution only the mayor supported; the last exchange with the terrorists had been insignificant except for their complaint about the amount of activity taking place near the exit from the catacombs; there had been no further communication with the Russians about the device.

"I know you really need information from the Russians to resolve the one-point safety issue. I'll let you know the minute I hear something," Giles said as he finished briefing Jean Denis.

Damned politicians, Jean Denis thought, spending all their resources trying to meet impossible ransom demands and making little effort to get the vital information that could make a difference. As usual, we're solving the wrong problem.

Glancing at his Rolex, one of the remaining vestiges of his free-spending bachelor days before Christine and the twins, Jean Denis realized it had been well more than two hours since the EOD team had departed for the

Working Point. There had been no news. He was not surprised, because he knew that people engaged in response activities can become so focused on the task at hand that they become oblivious to everything else. But he was a little annoyed, because he'd made it a point to ask the commander to check in. At that moment, Pierre materialized at his side, holding out the phone connected to the Working Point.

"Commander? What's going on?"

"We've successfully drilled the first hole. We didn't hit any mesh or set anything off. We're about to insert the probe and take a look inside. We'd like to drill the second hole at the same time, in order to save time. What do you think?"

"I think that you're right, we need a different look, but I'm still concerned about what the drill might hit. Let's hold off on the second hole until we've seen a few of those pictures from the probe."

"I really think we should go ahead and drill that other hole. If we don't, we're wasting some valuable time."

"I don't disagree. Maybe I'm being overly cautious, but I'd like to hold off."

"As you wish, Jean Denis, but I think it's a mistake. I'll call you back just as soon as we get the first pictures."

"Thank you, sir," Jean Denis replied as he hung up. He hoped his conservatism would not prove disastrous. His anxiety accelerated as he personally surveyed the status of the X-ray equipment. The gleaming, new high-energy device they had been awaiting for eighteen months sat slumped in a corner of the room, one corner of the shining machine crushed where it had been dropped while being unloaded. The entire diagnostic crew looked disheartened and embarrassed as they prepared their sole remaining resource, the lower-energy 1980s-vintage diagnostic dinosaur. Jean Denis knew that the team's chances of getting anything useful were slim, and his first impulse was to tell them to forget it and wait for the Americans. But there was no way he could do that to them—they were already feeling miserable—and he did not want to add to their embarrassment. Plus, there was plenty of time left before the Americans were due to arrive, and possibly the under-energized machine could provide information that would be useful in the next phases of the operation.

"You guys could be up very soon. How's it looking?" he asked no one in particular, not being able to find the team leader.

"This baby is ready to go. From the trials we've just concluded, it's never operated better. Whether or not it's up to the task remains to be seen. And, Jean Denis, we are so sorry—"

"Forget it," Jean Denis interrupted. "These things happen. The thing we need to concentrate on is getting the best data we can with what we have to work with. How many of you guys are going down?"

"Well, we'd planned on four," the team leader answered, having suddenly materialized.

"Four? Do you really need that many people?"

"That's what we had planned."

"Too many," responded Jean Denis. "I think it's questionable how much useful information we'll get and I don't want the risk any higher than absolutely necessary. Can you possibly do it with three?"

Reluctantly, the team leader nodded.

"Good. Now what are your plans?"

"We have eight cassettes ready to go. Our plan is to take an upper and lower image at four different horizontal locations; we think that we can cover the entire device with these. We hope that a fifteen minute exposure at each location will be enough to give us some resolution."

Jean Denis interrupted. "What do you think about doing just a single horizontal sweep along the center-line and doubling the exposure time?"

After some hesitation, the team leader acknowledged that the improved resolution could compensate for the decreased coverage. "Okay, let's do it. If we don't encounter any problems, Jean Denis, we could have some pictures developed and ready for you well before noon, when the Americans get here. This schedule might slip a bit with three people rather than four, but we should be able to do it in three hours or slightly more."

"But not hurrying so much that you compromise safety?" Jean Denis prompted.

"No, you can bet we'll give that device all the respect it deserves," the leader reassured him.

"Good luck. Get us something to work with. The police are keeping tight control down there, and we want to keep the visibility of the operation as low as possible since it looks like the terrorists are watching the entrance. I will let you know when the stage is yours. Please don't forget we want to know what is happening."

"We will. I'm more optimistic about what we can do with this old machine than a lot of these guys are."

After watching the diagnostic team load their equipment and head for the Working Point, Jean Denis returned up front where Pierre was gesturing to him with a group of fuzzy eight by twelve centimeter images.

"The EOD people sent some pictures. The commander says that you're not going to believe them and to call as soon as you've looked them over. He isn't sure what they should do next. And I have to tell you: I've looked at them and I don't have any idea what we're looking at either."

Examining the pictures, Jean Denis could readily identify the body of an artillery shell from the rotating band forward to where the ogive usually attached. Instead of the ogive, there was a metallic structure extending almost a full meter forward of the cylindrical shell body. What was totally puzzling was the large assortment of haphazardly positioned wires running in and out of this forward casing and throughout the whole interior of the wooden crate; it looked like an intricate spider web.

"Just what the hell is all of that in the interior of the shell? Are they strings? Electrical wires? I don't understand," Jean Denis asked the commander as soon as he had him on the phone.

"We're not quite sure either. They do look like wires and some of them look like they're connected to the sides of the wooden crate. Maybe it's either a real or sham anti-intrusion system. Some of them seem to go nowhere. Can you see all of the holes in that front casing? It almost looks like a punchboard. You can see some wires that go into it, and then I'd swear the same wire seems to emerge through a different hole. We've never seen anything like it, and none of us has any idea what they might be doing; our best guess is that it's just a complicated ruse. We can't see anything that might be a detonator cable; we assume all of that kind of stuff might be enclosed in the interior of that forward casing. We have no idea where the firing set might be, and obviously any attempt to defeat this thing by explosively isolating the firing set from the device itself is off the table unless we get much better pictures. We looked closely to see if we could identify anything that looked like an antenna on the device and, as someone said, there could be none or there could be twenty. We'd really like to drill that other hole on the back side of the crate and see if that provides any clearer information."

"Don't do anything right now. I'm worried about the time it will take to drill the second hole and I question if pictures from a different angle are going to give us much more than we already have. Let us discuss it up here and get back to you within fifteen minutes. In the meantime, could you reinsert that probe and try and get some more pictures through that same hole? They might prove helpful."

"Okay, Jean Denis, it's your call. We really don't know what these clowns have done."

Summoning the disablement and containment leaders along with Aimon, the diagnostician who had not gone to the Working Point, Jean Denis and Pierre laid out the pictures from the EOD scope and reviewed what the commander had told them. Recognizing that any additional time allocated to the EOD to drill a second hole probably wouldn't provide much additional information and would reduce the time available for the X-ray exposures, the group collectively decided that there was little to be gained by drilling the second observation hole.

The commander expressed disbelief, displeasure, and then anger when Jean Denis explained the decision. Once again he signed off the phone call by saying "it's your call," but this time the intonation of the phrase was totally different.

Within twenty minutes, the diagnostic team leader called from the Working Point and told Jean Denis that his team was in place and ready to take their first exposure. "Good, keep us informed. Let us know as soon as you get the first shot developed so we can decide if there's any reason to continue."

With the diagnostics started, Jean Denis began fielding the inevitable phone calls from the command post. He'd been waiting for them; he was seasoned enough to realize that during any disaster a certain number of people who join the response team don't have any real role or any real power. In order to justify their presence, these functionaries attempt to seize any bit of available information from the people at the Working Point, the people who are already overloaded with responsibility. Within an hour, three different bureaucrats had called to see if there were any updates on the effects predictions. Each time, Jean Denis dutifully walked down to the effects prediction area in search of new information.

"Doesn't it just figure," he grumbled to himself, "they keep wanting better data but the biggest uncertainty is the prediction of the yield. They could be useful and really push for that information but only at the risk of incurring someone's displeasure. So, to avoid that, they just keep asking me for the same information over and over."

The effects gurus kept telling him the same thing: if they were able to detonate the HE and keep the device from going nuclear, it was probable that everything could be contained within the confines of the catacombs. If, however, a nuclear yield of fifty to one hundred tons occurred, the cavity would vent and Paris would be exposed to a devastating radioactive cloud. If this were to occur, buildings within one hundred meters of Ground Zero would probably be damaged. Assuming that the yield was not over one hundred tons, they were comfortable not evacuating people outside a half-kilometer radius, but neither analyst was willing to estimate what size yield would not produce a radioactive cloud outside the catacombs.

Well, Jean Denis thought, I'll forward this up even though it's no different than what we sent an hour ago. It will give them another opportunity to vent about the unwillingness of conservative scientists to provide the information that they need. Maybe they'll be so busy venting and discouraged by the lack of updated data they won't bother to call again.

Realizing that Giles was at the command post earning every franc of his salary, Jean Denis allowed himself a smile. He would make his superior's job even a little harder. "Giles?" he asked when someone picked up the phone at the CP.

"Go ahead, Jean Denis," Giles responded a moment later.

"Could you help keep those clowns off our back? They keep asking for better effects calculations, three different requests in the last hour. Not only can we not do any better than what they already have, whatever we tell them won't make any difference. The size of the evacuation will be governed by how many people they can move out in the time available; a 20 percent or so difference in our prediction won't make any difference. We've got plenty to do without babysitting them. If a release should occur, we'll make calculations of the cloud path and behavior just as soon as we can but, for now, please try to get your friends off our backs."

"I understand, Jean Denis, but please believe me when I tell you that I'm not having much more fun trying to control the idiots than you are. And, at this point, I'm not sure that I have any friends."

"Oh, I'm sorry. I had imagined that you guys were sitting around in a circle up there, feet up on the table, telling war stories, drinking wine, and flipping a coin to see whose turn it was to call Jean Denis." Then, continuing on a more serious note, he added, "It's getting pretty stressful down here, so I'd appreciate it if you would do what you can. I promise that I'll let you know when I have more news."

As Jean Denis put down the phone, he again glanced at his watch. "Pierre. You'd better grab your entourage and get out to the airport. Someone needs to meet the Americans. Now, Aimon, what is it you have?"

"The first X-ray image," Aimon answered, handing Jean Denis a fuzzy photonegative.

They placed the film in the reader and, together, moved in closer to study it. The image was taken from near the rear end of the crate and, as expected, all they could discern was the rear of a dense, approximately one hundred and fifty millimeter diameter cylinder. That was it, the X-rays hadn't come close to penetrating the metal.

"This doesn't tell us much of anything we didn't know," Aimon groused.

"You're right. I hope by now they've moved forward of that heavy case. Call down and make sure they have—we don't need to waste any more time duplicating this shot, it's almost useless."

Shortly, Aimon was back with several images taken near the front of the crate. While no specific components could be identified, the delineation of individual structures was much greater. It was easy to determine where the case of the shell ended and where the more transparent front shield began.

It was even possible to distinguish, although not identify, a mishmash of components inside the lighter metal shield.

"Now that's more like it," Jean Denis exclaimed after they'd taken a close look at the film, feeling that his group's skill was somewhat vindicated. "A couple more like this and hopefully we'll have a better idea of what we're dealing with."

The courier arrived with the next image before Jean Denis could finish his fresh cup of coffee. This time they could see something completely unexpected: an unusual dense, rectangular object almost entirely filling the shield at the forward edge of the frame.

Subsequent images, when they arrived later, mapped the entire length of the weapon. The dense object extended nearly thirty centimeters, filling the entire front portion of the metallic enclosure. Jean Denis and everyone who had gathered around the viewing screen looked at one another in silent shock. They had never seen a component like this in any nuclear weapon—what the hell was it?

CHAPTER FOUR
Bison
Tuesday, September 12, 1995

Someone woke Bison with a cup of lukewarm, milky coffee shortly before the Dassault landed at Charles de Gaulle. It was gloomy and damp again in the City of Lights, definitely not Office du Tourisme weather. When the rumpled scientists deplaned, they found themselves in the midst of a contingent of chattering Frenchmen. Bison was straightening his jacket, trying to get his bearings when he was smothered by Pierre's bearish frame. The bighearted hug put to rest any fears he had about the American advisors possibly being forced upon their French counterparts.

Pierre's greeting was indifferent compared to Jean Denis's excitement when the police convoy delivered the scientists to the assembly point. "You'll never know what your being here means to me, Bise," he said as he reached up to kiss his old friend on both cheeks. Gesturing to all the Americans, "I'm glad to see all of you. Spend a few minutes freshening up while we unload your equipment, and then we'll meet back here and I'll let you know what's going on."

As soon as the equipment that was needed immediately was unpacked, and the nitrogen cooling of the diagnostic detectors was underway, Jean Denis began briefing the entire scientific team.

He started by pointing out the location of the device in the catacombs on a wall map, and then explained the chlorine spill cover story and the evacuation efforts which affected everyone within two kilometers of the spill.

"So that's where the device is located and how we've explained the evacuation. We desperately need to figure out more about that device. We're going to repeat the passive screening with the American detectors to identify

94

exactly where the nuclear material is positioned and to reconfirm that we're dealing with a plutonium weapon."

Turning to Aimon's diagram, he went on, explaining the wild array of wires or strings which the EOD had observed and that the preliminary X-rays had them completely perplexed. Turning to point to the diagram "Here we see a thin metal structure attached to an artillery shell. Inside the metal structure you can see fusing and firing components and here an unidentifiable, dense object about thirty centimeters in length. We have no idea what this object is. After we repeat the passive screening that I mentioned, I'd like to get the American high-energy X-ray gear in place. Hopefully, those images will help us determine exactly what it is that we are dealing with. If they don't, we may have to risk using the Cobalt-60 source the Americans brought over."

Standing off to the side, Bison surveyed the thirty scientists listening to Jean Denis. He wondered how many of them realized that the "risk" involved with the Cobalt-60 meant the possibility of accidental activation of some electronic circuitry in the device due to the high energy and high intensity of the Cobalt's gamma rays. He winced inwardly at the severity of the situation and turned back to listen to Jean Denis, who was explaining that efforts to ascertain the origins of the artillery shell were proving fruitless.

"Our embassy has been in contact with the Russian bureaucracy. The Russians still insist that all their weapons are accounted for, that they are all securely stored, and that the last of their artillery shells was retired years ago. They appear to be quite offended by any suggestion that it could be a Russian weapon, and say that we are most likely dealing with a stolen American weapon. When asked if, on the off chance it is a Russian weapon, whether it would be one-point safe, the Russian bureaucrat heatedly insisted that their weapons had always been designed with safety as the foremost consideration. Then he hung up. I think I speak for everyone concerned when I say that I personally don't find that answer very comforting. In short, we have no assurance that that weapon is one-point safe.

"So, that's everything we don't know," Jean Denis summarized with a wry smile. "Here's what we do know." He went on to summarize the tentative timeline for the entire response sequence. By 2:00 am the next morning, all diagnostics would be completed. The scientific team would then formulate a plan for disabling the device and submit the plan to the prefect of police no later than 4:00 am.

"It's crucial that they accept or reject our plan within two hours. We'll stress that if they take longer than two hours to make a decision they will be putting the lives of people at the Working Point in jeopardy. If they reject our plan, there won't be time to formulate a second plan; we may simply have to forgo the scientific option. Once we finally get their approval, and assuming that we do, we will have about six hours to set up whatever system we are going to use. This system needs to be in place, and ready by 2:00 pm. That will be cutting it perilously close to the announced detonation time of 5:00 pm. I really don't trust that detonation time: historically, the accuracy and reliability of terrorist's timers and firing circuitry have proven to be highly unreliable. On a further happy note, if the terrorists see a lot of equipment moving around on Remy Dumoncel, they may have the capability of detonating the device early.

"One other thing. And this is crucial. You Americans are here as consultants only, and you need to adhere to this. We need your advice on how to set up your equipment, how to properly align it, what to change to get clearer results and how to interpret the data. But according to the agreement we made when we asked for your assistance, there will be no hands-on; none of you is authorized to go to Ground Zero. There are clear channels of communication set up between here and Ground Zero. You will use those, but you may not go to the Working Point. Are there any questions?"

One, two, three ... Bison counted to himself, *and here we go...* as one of the American diagnosticians' hands shot into the air. "Jean Denis," the man asked, "What if we want to go to Ground Zero to make sure our equipment is set up correctly? Or what if it doesn't work properly once it's down there?"

The questions brought the rudiments of a smile to Jean Denis's fatigued face. "I knew one of you guys would ask that. But the agreement is that no Americans will go to the Working Point. None. No one. Not even for five minutes. I need that to be perfectly clear. Any deviation of this policy will require the explicit approval of Admiral Grangly and the prefect. I'm sorry, but that was the deal. Now let's get started."

The scientists dispersed into their work teams, with the Americans grumbling among themselves about the Ground Zero policy. They had understood the policy when they had been recruited, but it was one thing when they were thousands of miles away and completely different now that they were within a mile of the problem.

Bison found the nearest phone and called Admiral Grangly. "I've got some very unhappy scientists on my hands. The Ground Zero policy is going to be a big problem. These guys have spent years developing their specialized equipment, and they're not happy turning it over to people who've never even seen it, let alone used it. They don't want to be blamed if someone uses it incorrectly. Their pride and the judgment of their technical competence are at stake. I can't blame them for being upset."

"Do you want me to make a decision right now?"

"I thought I did when I called, but now I'm thinking it should be a joint Federal-Lab decision. I'll talk to the guys here if you will consult with the people up there and the prefect. I'll call back shortly, and we can talk some more."

"Okay, Bise, sounds like a plan."

Bison spoke to each of his men individually, and the decision was unanimous. Each scientist knew it meant accepting greater risk, and each was anxious to accept it and get started.

Bison was proud of his team. He was not sure he would have been as brave as they were being but decided not to share that information. When he called the admiral back, he learned that the headquarters contingent had all agreed that it was reasonable to allow the Americans to participate at Ground Zero. He knew that this decision would be widely applauded if everything worked out; he also knew who would be the inevitable scapegoat if it didn't.

"Keep me posted, Bise," the admiral directed. "I'll call each of the lab directors and give them the update, and I'll be sure to let them know the change in action level was a unanimous decision. I'm really proud of you guys. In the military we command people to undertake dangerous assignments; you and your team of civilians didn't have to be commanded, you volunteered. That's impressive."

While Bison was talking to the admiral, the passive diagnostic team of two French engineers and one American had gone to the Working Point to determine if the device contained plutonium and, if so, to locate the nuclear sphere within the crate. The remaining American diagnostician was preparing the X-ray equipment and instructing his French counterparts in its use. "We'll be ready to go the minute the passive guys get back," he assured Jean Denis and Bison.

The French effects scientist was more upbeat than when Jean Denis and Bison previously approached his station. Amid the whirring effects-prediction computers and damage-contour plots flying out of printers, he looked up at his superiors. "Not much is changing; the American calculations agree pretty well with ours: if the nuclear yield is a few tons or greater, the thing is going to vent. The Americans believe the major damage radius might be as small as one hundred and sixty meters. They also agree with us that if the disablement limits the output to only the HE yield, the effects can be contained within the catacombs."

"Great job," Jean Denis replied. He gestured to a large conference table on one side of the vast room. "I'll call these predictions into Giles, and then Bison and I will be over at that table if you get any new calculations."

As Jean Denis and Bison took their seats at the table, Jean Denis turned to his old friend. "I've got something that I need to discuss with you. I need a favor. A really big favor, one I probably should not even request. But I need to. Would you be willing to be the Scientific Commander at the Working Point during the disablement/containment phase until the problem is resolved? I originally planned to do it myself, but I've concluded that it won't be possible to both coordinate the operation at the Working Point and deal with the people at the command point. I've thought about asking Pierre to do it, but he just doesn't command enough respect when things get dicey—he's too French, he gets too emotional in tough situations. You're much cooler. Actually, you're the best choice of the three of us. I'll understand if you don't want to do it, and you're certainly not under any obligation."

Damn it, Bison thought. He knew Jean Denis's assessment of the three men's temperaments and abilities was correct. He agreed that he was probably the right person for the job. He also knew he did not want to face the danger the situation presented, and he had promised Bev he would not put himself at risk. But how could he refuse the dangerous job after his men had just volunteered so readily? What is leadership anyhow?

"Of course," he heard himself saying after a moment's pause. "I'd be flattered to do it."

"Thank you," Jean Denis replied, casting a long look at his friend, acknowledging both the complexity of the decision and his gratitude for the affirmative answer.

• • •

Bison was sitting by himself at the conference table, looking at the most recent X-ray images when Jean Denis returned from reporting the current Working Point roster to Giles. Jean Denis's face was vivid with anger, and he was spewing a combination of French and English so fast that Bison could not follow him. Eventually Bison was able to grasp that there had been another conversation with a Russian official who had been intentionally unhelpful, arrogant, and rude.

"I can't understand it," Jean Denis sputtered as he calmed down. "The Russians refuse to give us any information that might help. They know that the Soviet Union and America were the only countries that ever produced more than a few nuclear artillery shells. And they know that the world knows their weapon accountability was a joke after the dissolution of the Soviet Union. I'm willing to bet my life that that device in the catacombs in one of theirs. Why can't they cooperate? Why won't they give us information about design? All they have to do is tell us if their artillery shells were one-point safe. I don't want to hear 'our weapons are designed to the latest modern safety principles'! I want to hear 'our 152mm artillery shells are one-point safe'!"

Bison interrupted Jean Denis' tirade. "I know, I understand your frustration. But think about it. You know how difficult it is to design an explosive lens system that will achieve simultaneous implosion. It's particularly true for a small device—like an artillery shell—that can contain only a minimal amount of explosive. The weapon in the catacombs, wherever it came from, is almost certainly one-point safe."

"You know that, Bise, and I know that," Jean Denis replied, calming down. "But the people upstairs aren't going to buy it or don't want to hear 'probably.' They're skeptical of any technical solution at this point, and hypotheticals aren't going to cut it."

"I know, but let me tell you something else." Bison went on to remind Jean Denis about Senator Sam Nunn's Cooperative Threat Reduction program, established with the Russians right after the Soviet Union dissolved. The main purpose of the CTR program was to help dismantle the Soviet Union's nuclear arsenal, but there was also money set aside to fund research projects by the newly unemployed Russian scientists. The hope was that the scientists would be so busy researching that they wouldn't be tempted to apply their knowledge and skills to establish nuclear weapons programs in non-nuclear countries. In the early days, as the program was being designed, there was a series of scientist-to-scientist exchanges in an attempt to identify useful research projects for the Russian scientists.

"It was an interesting time, Jean Denis. We were getting to talk to people on the other side that had spent twenty years working on the same problems we had been investigating. The politicians demanded that we not share weapons information, but let's be honest: people who have worked a long time on solving particular problems are almost incapable of not discussing their solutions with others who have been laboring over the same questions. So, of course, it happened a bit. During one of the formal discussion sessions, when I thought things had mellowed to the 'we're all best buddies' stage, I asked whether the Soviet weapon designers had paid any attention to one-point safety. Once again, I had stepped into it. The room became silent, and I felt dozens of eyes drilling into me; I can't imagine why I have a reputation for blundering outspokenness. Finally, the head of the Russian delegation, a bear of a general, responded, ice dripping from his words, 'All of our weapons are built to modern safety practices.' With that, that discussion came to an abrupt end.

"The routine during these conferences was for the evening to be spent in cocktail parties and dinners. A big part of the cultural exchange was the Russians goading their new American friends into vodka drinking contests. The evening after my indelicate question, a Russian scientist with whom I'd developed a several hundred thousand dollar proposal for a research project called me over to a quiet corner during the customary vodka-fest.

"He apologized for his general's rudeness, recognized why I had that particular concern, and assured me that every Soviet weapon produced after the mid 1980s was certified to produce essentially zero yield with a single-point initiation. I reported this conversation in my after-conference report. No one ever mentioned it, and my guess is that no one ever read it. But his sincerity completely convinced me and I would bet almost anything that if the device in the catacombs is Russian—and what else could it be?—that it is one-point safe."

"Thank God," Jean Denis sighed, visibly relieved. "I need to go tell Giles about this and see what he wants to do with this information. It's second-hand information, but you're obviously convinced and, at that juncture, I can't see any apparent reason for the fellow not to be truthful. I don't know if this will affect the decisions at command center or not, but they certainly should be aware of it."

Just after Jean Denis departed for the command center to relate Bison's story, Pierre called from the Working Point.

"It is plutonium, Bison. We managed to get pretty distinguishable americium signals both along the axis of the device and again near the open end where there is less shielding. We want another half hour to see if we can determine precisely where the core of the device is located along the longitudinal axis. If you want to send the X-ray people down now, they can start getting set up without interfering with us."

"Good idea. Jean Denis has gone to the command center, but I'm sure he'd agree with that plan."

"Thanks, Bise. The sooner I get out of here the better. It's creepy down here."

"I'll bet," Bison responded, thinking that he would soon experience firsthand just how creepy it was.

Jean Denis was disheartened when he returned. Command center was in chaos; not only would the terrorists not extend the deadline, they were threatening to move zero time ahead. The people upstairs had come to the conclusion, from conversing with the terrorists, that the terrorists had some method of communicating with the device. Jean Denis explained that no suspicious signal had been found, just the mysterious wires inside the metal structure attached to the shell, and the police decided that one of the wires must be an antenna and, if so, it should be removed immediately.

"They're interested in your story, but they're too busy grasping at straws to think about anything right now. They said they may want to hear it from you themselves 'at a more appropriate time.' I'm just glad to be back down here. Why don't you go grab some food and try to sleep while we wait for the X-rays? I'll call you if anything happens."

"Good idea." Bison looked at his watch. It was 5:00 pm. Twenty-four hours till zero hour.

• • •

The dry cornstalks made an eerie rustling noise as he crashed through them. Someone was behind him, hollering, but he kept running. The burlap bag containing the two small watermelons was really heavy, but he could not stop. "Where are Jack and Cliff? What's that awful noise? Is my leg bleeding? Oh, my God, was that a gunshot? Who's calling me?"

"Bison, Bison, where are you?" Bison recognized his name, heard someone calling him, but did not recognize the voice. "Bison! Are you awake?" the voice persisted.

He bolted upright. He was not in a cornfield. Where was he? Right, he was in Paris. There was a possible nuclear weapon. He needed to wake up. His mind racing, he managed to stammer, "Has something happened?"

"No, but the photos have come back from the Working Point. Jean Denis thought you'd like to see them as soon as possible."

"I'll be right there." Bison washed his face and brushed his teeth in the sink in his little cubicle, got dressed, and threw a lingering gaze at the bottle of red wine on his bedside table. "I'll be back soon," he promised the bottle. Then he stopped. Would he be back soon? What was about to happen? Was this the last time he would ever go through the getting-up process? He thought longingly of Bev and the kids. *"Stop it,"* he told himself. *"This is no time for that kind of nonsense. Just get on with it."*

Everyone, including some French military personnel he had never seen before, was huddled around the light table.

"Ah, my good friend has joined us. Did you have pleasant dreams?" a rumpled Jean Denis, who obviously had not had any sleep, asked. "You'll find these images quite intriguing. But first, we have some terrific news about the radio link the terrorists installed to communicate with the weapon.

"The diagnosticians found a transmitter hidden in a crevice near the exit door. This is probably a backup to the internal timer in the weapon; they can use this transmitter to detonate early if they need to. We obviously don't want them to be able to detonate while we're down there working, but we can't simply destroy their communication link because it may be set up to fire should it be disrupted. We've decided to take control of the system; we will carefully monitor the signal for several hours, and set up a duplicate transmitter under our control to broadcast the identical signal. When we're convinced that our system duplicates theirs, we will remove their transmitter. We're currently monitoring the entire RF spectrum in the catacombs and are working on the substitute transmitter."

"That is good news," Bison responded. "I think we'd all vote for no early detonations. What do the new pictures look like?"

The new images did not show much detail near the rear of the shell, with the thick shell casing proving almost impenetrable to even the high energy X-rays. Looking closely, he could see a dark circular region three or four inches in diameter toward the longitudinal middle of the shell.

"I'm sure you've concluded that is the pit?" he asked no one in particular. Murmurs of assent answered.

The components in the front of the shell were much clearer in these images than they had been in the previous X-rays. A montage of the devices' fusing and firing circuitry was clearly visible but, with everything superimposed on top of one another, it was almost impossible to identify any individual components.

"Just what is that?" Bison asked, pointing to a dense area laced by surface striations and pinholes at the very front of the assembly. This time no one ventured an answer. Irrational silence.

"No one is even willing to make a guess? Okay then, that will have to wait. Has it been determined what we do next?"

Again, no answer.

"C'mon folks, we need a plan. Let's take a few minutes, everyone take another look at the images, and then we'll try to figure out what we're dealing with here. Honestly, I don't have any ideas either. What about you, Jean Denis?"

Jean Denis looked even wearier than he had just a moment earlier. "I'm baffled. I don't know why they'd incorporate anything so massive into the system. As it stands right now, I think we really have only two options: go back and get X-rays from a different orientation to try and figure out what that blob is, or use the Cobalt source to get greater penetrability. Does anyone have any other ideas?"

"Excuse me, sir, but I just realized what that dark item might be."

Everyone, including Bison, turned excitedly to see that the speaker was one of the soldiers that Bison hadn't been able to identify a few minutes earlier.

"If I'm not mistaken, those are two of the twenty-eight volt, two hundred and fifty amp-hour NiCad batteries that we have used for years in our telemetry systems."

Everyone looked back at the film. "Damn, I think he's right," Jean Denis exclaimed. "And those are the wires and holes that the EOD folks saw earlier." He paused for several seconds, thinking. "But why do they need so much power? And why two of them?"

"Oh, my God," a half-dozen voices gasped almost simultaneously. "That thing is armed!"

The entire warehouse seemed instantaneously to pulsate with fear and despair. If the firing set was already armed, any inadvertent RF signal or even a simple jarring of the device could cause the trigger circuitry to function and the device to detonate. In usual circumstances, working around armed explosives was absolutely prohibited; here, unfortunately, everyone realized there was no alternative. The complexion of the game had changed; it suddenly had become much more dangerous.

"Well, at least that makes our decision easier," Jean Denis muttered to Bison. Bison nodded back, exchanging a knowing but troubled look with his friend. While it was probably safe to take more X-rays—they'd already done that successfully—exposing the possibly radiation-sensitive electronics in the firing system to the much more energetic gamma source such as Cobalt-60 was a risk that neither Jean Denis or Bison was prepared to take.

"Any suggestions?" Jean Denis asked, somewhat as a courtesy, to see if the others gathered around the table concurred with what he and Bison had tacitly accepted to be the most appropriate course of action.

"I think it's clear that we shouldn't take the Cobalt source down there," Pierre answered, "it's just too chancy. We might get better pictures, but I think we already know what our proposed solution is going to be. A better use of our time would be to take some vertical X-rays to verify if those indeed are NiCad batteries."

"I agree," Aimon interjected. "If that firing set is charged, I also would suggest that we can no longer consider disabling that device by attacking the firing set. I don't believe there is any reliable way to destroy that capacitor before it has a chance to dump its charge into the detonators."

The suddenly solemn group murmured agreement.

"Anything else?" Jean Denis asked.

Someone from the back of the room spoke up. "It is going to be a pretty perilous operation getting that X-ray source aligned above the device in order to get good images, particularly with a charged firing set."

"I agree," Pierre concurred. "We will have to build some type of sturdy structure to solve that problem. But do we still feel that it's worth the risk to try and get those vertical X-rays?" No one spoke against continuing with the previously agreed-upon plan.

"Bison, do you have anything else?" Jean Denis finally asked.

"No, I completely agree. Let's get on with it. Let's try not to even touch that crate, the thing is just begging to detonate."

Turning back to the group, Jean Denis continued. "Okay, I think we've got a plan. You have about five hours of your allotted time frame remaining. Try and get us some good vertical X-rays. But do not take any unreasonable chances. We probably already know how we're going to attempt to disable this thing and these pictures most likely will not change that decision. So, Pierre, take your guys, build whatever fixture you think you'll need, go down and get some pictures and, for God's sake, be careful."

• • •

As the group disbanded, Jean Denis turned to Bison. "Sit down and let me fill you in on what's been happening up top while you were getting your beauty sleep. I went up there to talk to Giles and the admiral. They had talked to the prefect about your conversation regarding the one-point safety of Russian weapons. The admiral even remarked that he remembered reading it in your report. The prefect said that there was no need for you to come up and repeat it, he had no doubt of its authenticity, and he would inject it into the consideration whenever appropriate. But, for right now, no one seems at all interested in any scientific matters.

"The mayor and his cohorts are still dominating the debate in the Control Room. The mayor believes there will be an agreement with the terrorists; apparently he's delusional enough to think they will reduce their demands to just the prisoner releases and a lot more money, and not include the museum treasures. He wants all of the scientists out of the Working Point because having us there is agitating the terrorists. No one else seems to share his wishful thinking, but we do need to be more clandestine in coming and going to Working Point.

"They've been in contact with the Russian ambassador, attempting to get clarification of his 'modern weapon' statement, 'Of course, all of our weapons are one-point safe, it would be criminal to field any that aren't' is his most recent pronouncement. That's reassuring, but he's still unwilling to accept that the weapon could be one of theirs. He has announced that a nuclear terrorist incident is taking place in Paris to the Russian news media, but the story hasn't yet been picked up here in France. The traffic leaving the French Quarter right now is much heavier than usual for this time of the morning, which indicates that there may be a leak somewhere, but the city certainly hasn't yet reached a panic mode."

"Boss?" One of the French diagnosticians came up to where Bison and Jean Denis were sitting. "We've taken our most recent sketch of the device to the weapon designers. It is their guess, and they said to be sure to let you know that it's only a guess, is that the maximum yield that the device could have would be about fifty tons. They'll continue working on it and let you know if there is any significant change."

"Well that's good news. Thanks."

Bison turned to Jean Denis. "It will be a couple of hours before we get any of the vertical X-rays back. Go see if you can get some sleep. I'll let you know if anything happens. And keep your hands off of my wine."

Jean Denis smiled gratefully and was on his way to the bunk area before Bison finished his sentence. As he watched his younger friend walk away, Bison recalled the enjoyable times the two men had shared over the past decade. He thought about the time Jean Denis tried to hide his rented

Corvette from the police in Las Vegas after admitting, "I might have been going a bit fast" on I-15. And the dinner with Jean Denis and Christine at a small seaside restaurant outside of Bordeaux when the two teased Bison about "taking a bit of a dip," knowing damned well that the prudish Bison was not going anywhere near that water without a swimming suit. And he recalled the pleasure of the very relaxed dinner in a beautiful old cathedral/restaurant outside of Lyon where their elderly French and English companions relentlessly argued the relative merits of Cognac and Armagnac. Working together had certainly been a joy.

With things temporarily quiet, Bison called the admiral. No, the admiral informed him, the lab directors were not at all pleased with the active role their personnel were taking. "They all said that this was in direct contradiction to the agreement we'd made before you departed, that they would advise against it, and that it was something that we were going to have to iron out after we returned. Almost as if they'd rehearsed it, each of them reminded me that these laboratories were technical research organizations and not fire departments. They're just trying to cover their butts, Bise. It's my call, and I accept the responsibility."

"Thanks," Bison responded. "Jean Denis says it's a completely disorganized shouting match up there at command center."

"Oh, you know the French, loud voices, a lot of arm waving and posturing. The mayor wants to be heard, but I'm impressed with the job that the prefect is doing. But who knows what will happen when the prime minister gets here. I take it that you and Jean Denis's team are in complete agreement about how to dispose of the weapon?"

"There's no question in our minds, at this stage at least. We want to detonate it with a shaped charge and use the containment system."

"That's what I expected. Bise, please be careful when you're down there, I don't want to have to listen to your laboratory guys trying to absolve themselves of all responsibility if there's a catastrophe."

"I will, Admiral, thank you for your support."

"Oh, and Bise?"

"Yes, sir?"

"I'm afraid PJ's plane is stuck in Newark. There's a hailstorm. Try to do your best without him."

"Will do, sir."

After hanging up, Bison allowed himself the luxury of sitting back in the most comfortable chair he could find, closing his eyes, and waiting for the processing of the latest X-ray exposures.

CHAPTER FIVE
Bison
Wednesday, September 13, 1995
2:00 am

Bise was lying contentedly on a pristine sandy beach. Someone, he didn't know who, was gently rubbing some wonderful-smelling lotion over the tense muscles of his back; it felt great. He heard a noise and turned over to express his appreciation. There was no beach, there was no masseuse, there was only a very worried-sounding Jean Denis looking down on him.

"Are you okay, Bise?"

Bison faked alertness, somewhat ashamed for having fallen asleep again. "Yeah, I almost dozed off again. What's happening?" He surreptitiously checked his watch; it was almost 2:00 am. He had been asleep in that chair for more than an hour.

"The imaging team's on their way back with another set of X-rays, and they think they have the complete map of the signal pattern from the terrorist's external firing system. Our overall plan is still the same, and it will stay that way unless we see something strange in the new images. When we get the render-safe procedure solidified here, we'll present it to Giles, the admiral, and the prefect. Hopefully we won't have a large audience of politicians, because we need a quick decision, not a discourse on political philosophy."

Taking another look at Bison, Jean Denis yelled to the room at large. "Will someone please bring Bison a cup of coffee? I'm not sure he's with us. Americans don't seem to be able to stay awake after the sun goes down. That sludge in the bottom of the pot might do the trick."

The coffee and the diagnostic team arrived at the same time. Arranging the images on the light table and comparing them with the previous pictures, a three-dimensional perception of the component package began to take shape. The first thing everyone examined was the bulky devices at the front of the enclosure; without dissension, these were NiCad batteries. There was a buzz in the room: "That looks like a capacitor? Could that be the timer? What on earth are these? They don't look like transformers."

"Does anyone believe that we should attack the firing system?" Jean Denis asked.

Only negative responses.

"Well then, who wants to be the first to volunteer a plan?" he continued, knowing everyone there had probably come to the same conclusion but hoping that the strategy would originate with the players. Suddenly everyone wanted to talk, everyone was excitedly drawing sketches.

After making sure anyone who wanted to express an opinion had done so, Jean Denis interrupted the discussion. "We seem to all have about the same plan in mind, so let's go over it and make sure we're all in agreement. First, we need to get rid of the terrorists' ability to control the weapon. We'll replace their RF link with our own, giving us control of the device. This will eliminate the possibility of their activating the weapon while our disablement/containment crew is down there. There is a drawback in this: If we haven't properly captured the entire coded signal, the weapon could detonate during the transition. Also, there's another possible objection: we've eliminated the possibility of the terrorists turning off the weapon themselves. I don't think this is a strong concern, because we can always turn the link back on for them if it comes to that.

"The politicians are really concerned about the movement of people and equipment into and out of the exit door on Rue Remy Dumoncel. Apparently the terrorists have that door under surveillance, and they're raising hell about all the activity. Fortunately, that whole underground area where the device is located is riddled with connecting tunnels that were blocked off years ago by the government. Right now, the police are reopening one of the blocked tunnels that opens into the Port Mahon quarry. This will immediately become our new access point, our sole entrance into and out of the catacombs. We'll have to move the equipment further, and the passageways will be tighter, but this will alleviate concerns about the terrorists' worrying about what we're doing."

Turning to the police officer assigned by the provost to be the scientists' police liaison, "Brigadier, do you know how that operation is progressing?"

"The last I heard, the entrance had been opened, the tunnel was cleared to allow people to enter without crouching, and all the fire hoses, lighting, and communication alterations should be complete within a couple of hours.

We have people standing by to help move your equipment in whenever you say the word."

"Now!" Jean Denis commanded, turning back then to address the scientific team as he pointed to a schematic drawing. "I don't believe that the disablement/containment system we've chosen is going to surprise anyone. Bison referred to it earlier as Plan 1A. A one-kilogram shaped charge will be mounted on a short tripod, offset from the device crate by about a meter, and aimed to impact at the forward end HE ellipse. The tripod holding the shaped charge will be firmly staked to the ground so it will not move during the foaming operation. The firing set will be set about ten meters outside the containment structure with the detonator cable running under a water bag to the shaped charge. While the firing set can be activated on-site, in this situation the prefect will control firing of the detonator from the CP. When he pushes the button, it will send an encrypted signal to a receiver that I'll control in the quarry. We'll string a hard wire from my receiver to the firing set at Ground Zero. I don't know how you plan to cover all the entrances to the catacombs, brigadier, but we need to be sure that there are no tourists dawdling around in there when we set this thing off."

"We're already working on that, sir."

"Good. As I said earlier, we should have no problems setting this system up; it's our standard and we've probably done it a dozen times. There is a problem that we've run into on past operations, though; the containment system might muffle the explosion so that we can't tell for sure if a detonation has occurred or not. So we've devised a small diagnostic package that we'll insert next to the device. The package, which will contain radiation detectors and pressure gauges, will act as a monitor. Yes, Brigadier, what is it?"

"Excuse me, Jean Denis, but why don't you aim the shaped charge right at the middle of the explosive? Wouldn't that improve your chance of making sure that you hit the target?"

"Yes, our chances would improve, but the weapon designers say that hitting the middle of the explosive could have a higher probability of resulting in a nuclear detonation. And please, if anyone has a question as we go through this, feel free to interrupt."

When there was no response, Jean Denis looked at Bison. "Okay then, Bison, will you describe the containment system?"

Bison cleared his throat; he still had not managed to get the taste of that terrible coffee out of his mouth. "There's really not much more to say than has already been said. I think almost all of you have seen the twenty-five-foot containment cone we're going to use. Assuming we don't have a nuclear detonation, this system should confine all of the effects of the high explosive going off within the catacombs. If we fail in the process and have a nuclear event, it will be years before this section of Paris recovers.

"The major downside with using the foam containment is that the foams' useful life is between an hour and a half and two hours. After that, the water drains out and the ability of the remaining material to attenuate shockwaves and capture the particulate is compromised. So we want to generate it no longer than sixty to ninety minutes before the detonation. Also, since the generation process is more an art than a science, the foam technicians will remain at the Working Point as long as possible in case there are any last-minute refinements."

Pausing as he glanced about the room, he continued. "What I've just said might have come across as if using this system is a bit of a long shot. That is not the case. We have great confidence that this system will work well in this situation," he concluded with a nod toward Jean Denis.

"Thanks, Bise. Now we just have the evacuation process to consider. It's not our responsibility, but the prefect will use our advice to guide the evacuation of people who live or work near the vicinity of the device. The effects team has been massaging their calculations ever since they got here; their current proposal is that everyone within one hundred and fifty meters of Ground Zero should be evacuated immediately, and everyone out to four hundred meters should follow as time permits.

"If, for some reason, disablement and containment are not successful and a full-scale nuclear detonation occurs—please keep in mind that this is very much a worse-case situation—the team predicts a surface crater of ten- to twenty-meters deep with a radius of thirty to forty meters and a lip extending out as far as eighty meters. Most buildings within one hundred and fifty meters will probably be demolished, either by ground shock or the ensuing air blast. There should be little danger from the initial radiation because of the device's buried location, but there will be high-velocity ejecta from the cavity, including a lot of air-borne remnants of ancient Parisians. This material plus the longer-term blast wave will probably prove lethal for anyone within a one-hundred-meter radius.

"These effects, as serious as they might seem, will probably not be the greatest consequence. Cleanup will be. If the device goes nuclear, the cost of dealing with the anticipated radioactive contamination could easily be in the tens of billions of francs. When the cavity vents, and remember we're still talking about a full-scale nuclear detonation, a cloud of radioactive particulate will emerge, its height and trajectory dependent upon the local wind and thermal conditions at detonation time. Everyone in the city will be at risk from this contaminated cloud; therefore all Parisians should be prepared to wear some type of breathing protection. If the event goes nuclear, our effects team will become part of the prefect's staff. They will then become responsible for the real-time predictions of the cloud trajectory and behavior.

"That would be a truly calamitous outcome. If our disablement and containment are successful, as Bison has said, there should be no significant release of material outside the catacombs. We expect a lot of cracking but no significant destruction of the cavern walls. There will be a sludgy mess around the device, and everything will be covered with broken-down foam slurry. It will be essential to use sandbags to keep the drainage, which will be loaded with radioactive particulate, within the catacombs; it probably will be months before this tourist attraction can safely reopen. But Paris itself will be safe and there should be no loss of human life.

"A six-member team, three Frenchmen and three Americans, will emplace the disablement and containment systems and this team will remain at the Working Point until they are withdrawn by the prefect. Because of his previous experience, Bison will lead the group and Pierre will be his deputy. They will make any necessary on-the-spot decisions. Along with several other scientists, I will be stationed near the tunnel entrance in the quarry. I will have the receiver that, upon receipt of the signal from the command point, will relay this signal to the firing set. When Bison's team and my team leave here for the quarry, the rest of you are to await instructions from the command post."

• • •

Jean Denis and Bison had assumed that they would give their proposal to Giles and Admiral Grangly and then, after making any necessary refinements, take it to the prefect and his top staff. When they got to the prefecture, they discovered that the initial presentation audience would also include a conference room full of second level bureaucrats, most of whom had been anxiously waiting all day to participate in something.

"Damn, damn, damn, Giles," Jean Denis grumbled.

"I know, and I'm sorry." Giles consoled his subordinate. "There just wasn't any way to get out of it."

Bison understood Jean Denis's frustration but took some solace in the fact that PJ did not appear to have yet arrived. *That removes a major source of irrelevant questions,* he thought. Another annoyance presented itself when it became clear that the prefect was not ready to meet, and would not be for at least half an hour. More precious time was ticking away.

As Jean Denis and Bison milled about, waiting for the presentation to begin, they listened in on the conversations between the buzzing functionaries. Somehow, the terrorists seemed to be communicating in an untraceable manner with the French negotiators at least once an hour. As one of these conversations ended, the mayor jubilantly shouted, "We're getting there, we're getting there."

"They're willing to postpone, to give us a few more hours," one of the mayor's many aides shouted to no one in particular. "We've got to convince the damned Americans to step it up a bit with the prisoners and somehow get those obstinate English bastards to understand what right now means. If we all can focus on this just a bit, we can make it happen."

The mayor's staff and several of the city bureaucrats seemed to have formed a "Paris at Any Cost" alliance and were almost ready to declare victory. They were the only ones involved in the negotiations that had such enthusiasm for the supposed progress being made, one of the police negotiators told Jean Denis and Bison. He thought that the terrorists were just stringing the politicians along with no intention of granting a serious postponement of the deadline. So far, he explained, the ransom money had been increased by a factor of ten, and the return of the two colossal statues from the Louvre was off the table. The mayor was eager to transfer the money. Two of the three World Trade Center bombing participants were in a federal holding center in Denver, ready to be transferred to Le Sante Prison in Paris once the prime minister gave the go ahead. There was some extenuating circumstance on the release of the third prisoner but it was still being worked through diplomatic channels.

"The English won't go along," the police negotiator told them. "They won't give in to terrorists. Churchill once remarked that an appeaser is a person who keeps feeding a crocodile, hoping it will eat them last. They are adamant about not feeding the crocodile. The Brits, and I think this was probably tongue-in-cheek, suggested a trade of Mona Lisa for the Rosetta Stone, but the Louvre laughed at them. If the terrorists could humble the Americans a bit by forcing the return of the third prisoner, there might be a chance of settlement. But that would take several days, and I don't really believe the Americans are willing to cave in to the extortion either. I also don't think there's a chance in hell that the French police will ever accede to nuclear blackmail. But"—he grinned—"we are French, you know."

Finally everything was cleared away for Jean Denis to present the plan to Giles, the admiral, and everyone else crowded into the small conference room. Giles escorted Jean Denis and Bison to the three chairs reserved for them at the end of the conference table.

"Okay," he started, "it looks like everyone is here. We need this to go as quickly as possible as we're scheduled for an audience with the prefect. You will have a chance to comment, but please wait until after Jean Denis has completed his presentation. Jean Denis, go ahead."

"Our plan is rather simple. Many of you will recognize it from past exercises." He ignored the waving hands as he continued. When he finished his presentation and stopped for breath, the assault began.

"Wouldn't it be safer attacking the electronics?" was the first question.

"We don't believe so. First, from the X-rays we have, we can't positively identify which component is the firing set. Secondly, there are indications that the firing set is already charged. We'd be in a race for time, having to destroy the firing set before it dumped its energy into the detonators, and we aren't confident that we can win that race."

"Why is Bison leading the team?" came the next question.

"We considered our personnel, their experience, and what needs to be done. We've come up with what we feel is the best personnel fit. This decision has been very carefully deliberated. Next question?"

"Isn't removing their external triggering system pretty dangerous? What if they want to turn the device off?"

"Remember, we don't really know what that signal is for. If the terrorists demand that the link be activated, the people at Working Point will be in contact with the Command Center and they can reinstate the terrorists' control almost immediately. We want to get rid of that signal because it's frightening to be working around an armed device when someone who is not your friend holds the firing button."

"Have you considered such things as flooding the chamber, or freezing the device, or filling the area with petrol and burning the device?" asked one of the French desk-drivers, who apparently felt it advantageous to have his voice heard.

A flash of anger flickered across Jean Denis's tired face. "This solution is not something we have just drawn up today on the back of an envelope; we've been researching methods to defeat these types of devices for the better part of two decades. Yes, we have thought of those things and, in general, discarded them for their lack of utility. If you have some information that we don't possess that might support your suggestions, we'd be pleased to discuss them with you later, but this is obviously not the time. Are there any other questions?"

No one spoke; Jean Denis's anger had adjourned the meeting.

After some brief suggestions by both Giles and the admiral regarding the organization of the presentation and a slight, but smiling, reprimand by Giles to Jean Denis for his somewhat brusque response to the French bureaucrat, the group proceeded to its scheduled meeting with the prefect. Bison glanced nervously at his watch; it was now approaching 6:00 am, nearly two hours behind schedule but not yet approaching a critical juncture. The prefect's conference room was packed. Bison sensed this might prove difficult.

"Are we all here?" Giles questioned the prefect. Receiving a "I sure hope so" answer, he continued. "I'd like to have Jean Denis make his presentation, and then we will field any questions you may have."

"Not a chance," the vice-mayor shot back. "All this scientific crap should be suspended immediately. It's diverting attention from the real solution. We've just about got this problem solved; you scientists with your 'rendering safe' talk are making our job more complicated and making our adversaries question our intentions. I don't know why we're having this meeting and I suggest that we adjourn it and focus our attention on the only realistic solution."

"We're having this meeting because I requested it and because I believe that there's a lot of wishful thinking going on if you think that you're going to reach some type of satisfactory compromise with these terrorists," the prefect snapped angrily. "Need I point out to you that this is a police problem and, until I receive directions to the contrary from a higher authority, I intend to direct this operation? Please either remain quiet or excuse yourself from this room. Do I make myself clear?"

"Yes, sir," responded the questioner, resuming his seat while glancing at the mayor. Jean Denis restarted his presentation but got no further than the explanation of how the terrorists' communication link with the device was to be replaced by one of their own before the mayor himself was up and almost yelling.

"No, no, no. We can't do that. No way will we agree to have them lose their capability for controlling that device. They're about to agree to turn it off and you want to take away that capability? Ridiculous!"

The prefect stepped in. "I'm sorry, mayor, but you too are out of order. But I believe you do have a valid question. Do you have an answer for his concern, Jean Denis?"

"Yes, of course, sir. The team at the Working Point will be right there and have the capability to return that control to the terrorists at any time."

"I understand," responded the prefect. "But I think I agree with the mayor. Let's proceed and I'll make a decision on that point when the presentation is over."

Jean Denis finished the rest of the discussion without further interruption except for some muttered concern when he announced that Bison was the team leader. The instant he stopped talking the mayor was on his feet and yelling.

"I can't believe all of this scientific hocus-pocus. You guarantee nothing. You turn the future of Paris over to someone who is not even French. You've got to be kidding! Here we are on the threshold of reaching a very good settlement, and you're considering throwing it away on a long-shot pipedream. I never thought I'd see this day. I—"

"Enough! Enough! We've heard you, please sit down. Now!" The prefect was clearly about to lose his equilibrium.

Bison was not simply angry, he was furious. His attempt to stand was checked by the admiral's restraining hand on his shirttail. Everyone in the room probably saw the gesture and most probably knew exactly what he wanted to say: that not only was there a group of Americans here willing to risk their lives to assist the people of France, but he would remind them of Chateau-Thierry, of Normandy, of the France that was filled with graves of Americans who had died earlier this very century saving the country from tyranny, and now he and his compatriots were being treated with utter disrespect. That arrogant bastard!

Immediately another French voice spoke up, another civil servant Bison had not met. "I've heard Dr. Bison here plans on leaving the country immediately after the scientific team emerges from the catacombs. I don't like that idea. I believe that it's important that he stay here for the wrap-up meetings, particularly should something go wrong. He needs to be here to defend his decisions."

The prefect looked at Jean Denis questioningly.

Giles responded before Jean Denis had a chance to speak. "Bison's only daughter is getting married on Saturday. We specifically requested him to join us, and our agreement was—and I promised his wife as well—that he would be home in time for the festivities. Pierre will be at Ground Zero with the team, and I am confident he will be able to answer any questions that might arise. I do not see any overriding reason for Bison to be here once the operation is complete. Do you see something I'm missing?" he challenged the questioner. There was no response.

"Are there any more questions?" the prefect asked.

Another of the French ministers started to rise but thought better of it and sat back down, indicating that he would wait for the prefect's summation before making his statement.

"If not, let me tell you what I have decided. I see little reason why we cannot continue the render-safe effort in parallel with the diplomatic effort. The terrorists are concerned about all of the activity down on Remy Dumoncel so we've moved the access point to an entrance in the Port-Mahon Quarry, a move that we're making a major effort to keep out of the terrorists view. I tend to agree with the mayor about the terrorists' communication link; I will not approve substituting it, we'll just have to live with what we have there. I believe that we need to enhance our efforts at evacuating people in the immediate area of the device right now, even if it requires telling them that we have a nuclear threat to get them to move immediately. We need to keep working on these issues with the effects calculators; I want them to move up here immediately to the prefecture. If anyone has any severe disagreements with this plan, please stay after we adjourn here and we can discuss it and, if I agree with you, there's nothing here that we can't revise. Otherwise, this meeting is over. The plan is approved and we've got to let the implementers get started because they're nearly three hours behind schedule."

As they rose to go, Giles and the admiral pulled Jean Denis, Pierre, and Bison over to one side. Giles looked directly at each of the three scientists. "Be cool down there, guys. If anything unusual happens or if there's anything that becomes suspicious about the device, I want you, without hesitation, to get out of there immediately."

"And Bise," Giles said as they parted, "please disregard the 'he's not a Frenchman' comment; it was ridiculous and totally uncalled for."

Arrogant bastards, thought Bison as he mentally prepared to risk his life to help save their city.

CHAPTER SIX
Bison
Wednesday, September 13, 1995
10:00 am

Bison was still seething as he and Jean Denis drove back to the staging area. "C'mon, Bise, don't let the idiot mayor bother you. I've heard that his wife hasn't spoken to him for a year."

Bison looked incredulous.

"Yeah," Jean Denis continued, "she said she didn't want to interrupt him."

Bison permitted himself a glimmer of a smile, but he was still too angry to produce the famous full-out Bison grin.

Traffic on the streets was beginning to pick up. Bison didn't know if this was normal in the early morning hours or if the evacuation had actually started. There did seem to be more incessant sirens than usual and more empty buses moving toward the evacuation area; Bison hated to imagine how chaotic these streets would become in just a few hours. How ironic, he thought. I'd almost rather be in that cavern with the ticking bomb than out on these streets when pandemonium breaks loose.

He and Jean Denis quickly briefed the assemblage at the staging area, and then Bison, Pierre, and the rest of their six-man crew loaded into a police vehicle and departed for the quarry. Jean Denis and his three-man contingent were in a van right behind them, bringing the firing set relay system. As soon as they got to Working Point they would check the firing system. They wanted to be absolutely sure that the switch controlled by the prefect at command center triggered the receiver held by Jean Denis in the quarry and then was relayed to the firing set at the Working Point.

As they wound their way down into the quarry, Bison saw empty equipment pallets and glimpsed a foam generator being taken into the tunnel opening. His van stopped, and Jean Denis's vehicle pulled up right behind. The policeman in charge of the operation walked over to Jean Denis, speaking rapidly in French.

Jean Denis turned to Bison. "That's the last of the equipment," he said, gesturing toward the generator, "and they have already laid the hoses, and the cables for the voice communication and diagnostic system. So I think you're set."

Suddenly the policeman, who had begun to walk away, turned back toward the men, reached across Jean Denis, and extended his hand to Bison. Apparently not all Parisians shared the mayor's disdain for the American in charge of the dangerous operation.

Jean Denis pulled Bison aside as the entourage walked across the smooth, timeworn floor of the quarry toward the entrance to the catacombs. "This is where we part for now, old friend. I trust you know how special you've always been to me and Christine and that there is no one for whom I have greater respect. Please be careful in there and do whatever you think is right; no matter what transpires, your decision is my decision. But most of all take care of yourself and the rest of these guys; you're all very special people. And, in case you're concerned about it, that car will be right down here waiting for you when you come out."

After a quick hug, Bison turned away from his friend, and he, Pierre, and their four colleagues entered the dark tunnel.

They walked along the roughly hewn, graffiti-covered tunnel in silence, water dripping in the background. The atmosphere was quiescent, the air cool and somewhat rancid. The six men were solemn, proceeding in reverence to their dangerous mission, witnessed by the remains of the millions of Parisians interred in the walls. When they reached the Innocents chamber, they saw that the walls of the chamber were completely lined with neatly organized tibia and fibula interspersed with an occasional staring skull. It was eerily quiet. Looking around, it occurred to Bison that each of his men was praying.

It was then that Bison realized how comfortable he felt with his team. He could not have asked for anything better. Given the circumstances, these were exactly the guys he wanted by his side. And, in addition, it looked like all the equipment was in place, seemingly undamaged by its journey across the globe.

The presence of the familiar equipment was strangely reassuring. He had taken part in countless exercises, and he knew this equipment well. He trusted it. He had never, however, felt the need to trust it as much as he did at that moment, standing near an armed nuclear weapon.

Tearing his eyes from the comforting equipment, he cleared his throat and addressed his team. "Okay, let's get started. It's nearly 10:00 am and I'd like to see two things happen: I'd like to have everything ready to go by 2:00 pm and, secondly, I pray that the terrorists' timer is accurate. Let's try and clear a—"

His phone rang. Rolling his eyes at the team, Bison answered it with an aggravated, "Hello."

"Bise?"

"Yes, Giles, what is it?"

"You won't like this, but the mayor has demanded, and has browbeaten the prime minister and prefect into agreement, that we run a 'flat tire.'"

"What the hell is a flat tire?"

"Apparently the mayor was involved in some exercise where they checked out the entire firing system from the command post switch down to actually activating a simulated detonator; they called the test a flat tire. In his words, 'It was pretty neat.' I know, I know. But they're demanding one. Immediately."

"Oh, for Christ's sake. As if we didn't have enough to do. It's no big deal, we would do that anyway. Only we didn't have a cute name for it and I'd prefer doing it in the proper sequence. But we'll humor my dear friend. I'll let you know as soon as we get hooked up. Will he take our word for the result? I am an American, after all."

"Well, he wanted to send one of his dispensables—my word, not his—down there to observe, but we've managed to convince him to spare you that pleasure."

"Thanks for that small favor. We'll start right away; it'll probably take about fifteen minutes. Jean Denis, did you copy that?"

"Check, we'll hook everything up out here and turn it on and we'll be ready whenever you want to flat tire," Jean Denis responded with a smirk in his voice.

Bison turned back to the team in the catacomb. "I don't know if you guys followed all that, but we have to run a complete firing system check right now, something the mayor calls a flat tire. Michel, will you get out one of those dummy detonators, set up the firing set, and let me know when you're ready? In the meantime, let's get started building the protective structure to put over the device and clear everything out as well as we can to at least a five-meter radius from the device."

Paul and Henri each grabbed a hammer and some of the construction lumber that the police had carried in and started to build a temporary structure to protect the device box from jostling during the erection of the cone. Even though the rudimentary wooden frame was simple to build, it did not need to withstand the test of time since it would be removed when the cone was air-inflated. Bison heard Paul trying to explain to Henri that, based on long experience, it was best if Bison was not permitted to help with construction projects. The frame was nearly complete by the time Michel had set up the firing set and strung the detonator cable with the dummy detonator attached.

"Everything is ready here," Jean Denis's voice came over the communication system.

"And here," responded Michel, turning on the firing set.

"Okay then, Three! Two! One! Fire!" came an unfamiliar voice from the command point, followed almost instantaneously by the characteristic "pop" of the sugar-loaded dummy detonator.

"Looks good," Michel replied, followed by affirmation from Jean Denis and an unfamiliar voice that added, "Merci."

"That's it," Giles broke in.

"Anything else we can do for you?" Bison concluded, still slightly irritated at the mayor's insistent, unwelcome intrusion.

Finally it was time to unfold the fabric cone, a task that required all six men. The fabric was laid on the ground on the walkway and each man tugged on his section, pulling the fabric up and over the protective wooden framework and extending the edges out as far as possible within the confines of the cavern. Tubular water bags attached by straps sewn into the cone were then filled from the fire hose and fastened around the circumference of the cone; without the water bags, the bottomless structure would float away when the cone was foamed.

"Shall we go ahead and air it up, Bise?" Paul asked.

"I see no reason not to."

Paul and Henri zipped up the long, vertical access doors in the sides of the cone, attached a large exhaust fan to one the six-foot-long snouts that were sewn into the cone, turned on the exhaust fan, and the structure slowly raised within the confines of the cavern.

"Damn those guys," Bison muttered in half-hearted disgust as the cone began to rise. He looked at Paul, who was struggling to keep from laughing; seeing his delight, Bison himself was forced to laugh.

A female pinup with a striking resemblance to Madonna was painted on the side of the cone. The "artists," whom Bison fervently hoped were better engineers than artists, were the technicians charged with periodically inflating all the cones to make sure they remained in good condition. The last time Bison had seen their handiwork—that time in the form of Pamela Anderson—he had admonished them about wasting their time and talents on such endeavors. Apparently his lecture had not worked. He laughed to himself, realizing that the six men in the cavern that day would be the only people who would ever appreciate the technicians' meager creative talents.

Completely inflated, with Madonna extended to unrealistic proportions, the cone was an odd-looking structure. It pressed tightly against the cavity wall in the rear and ballooned out on the unconstrained sides. Paul and Henri opened one of the entrance zippers, stepped into the air-inflated cone, and disassembled the wooden protective form that they'd constructed over the device.

Reemerging, Paul announced, "We're done. It's your turn," he said, looking toward Alan and Michel who were waiting to emplace the disablement system.

It was almost noon.

The disablement equipment had already been unpacked and was ready to be moved inside the fabric structure. Alan and Michel worked quickly, carefully aligning the equipment so that the extremely high-velocity, molten-metal shaped-charge jet would traverse through the surrounding crate and strike the device in exactly the desired spot. After they were satisfied that everything was properly aligned, they securely staked down the tripod holding the shaped charge. After one last check of the entire system and the firing of another sugar-loaded dummy detonator, Alan and Michel left the structure, zipping up the door behind them.

Paul and Henri had already attached the two foam generators to the snouts in the cone and had connected them to the high-pressure water sources. They were presently tying a lanyard to the air vent at the top of the cone; without this exhaust, an air lock would occur and the cone would not inflate properly.

Calling Alan and Michel over to where he and Pierre were sitting, Bison said, "Well, guys, after you get the diagnostic system checked out, your part of this operation is over. All that will be left is to start the foaming and turn on the firing set. Pierre, Paul, Henri and I can handle that. I want you to leave when you're done. I don't want to risk any more lives than necessary."

Michel looked at Alan who, knowing what Michel was going to say, shook his head in silent agreement. "No, Bise, if you order us to leave we will, but we prefer to stay. We're part of this team. You stay, we stay. Maybe we can even help."

"Are you sure?" Bison asked, surprised but impressed by their loyalty.

"We stay," Alan told him with a pat on his shoulder.

"All right. It's your call. I really appreciate it. Thank you. You've made me proud," Bison said, rubbing his hand across his eyes.

"Okay, all ready down here," Bison reported to the teams at the command post and the quarry. "We are now going to eat our lunches and await guidance from you. Sooner rather than later would be good."

All six men found places to sit among the piles of bones, knowing that they were in for what could be a long and increasingly tense wait. It was now ten minutes after 2:00 pm.

• • •

While Bison and his team anxiously awaited their instructions from above, the decision-makers were no closer to reaching a conclusion than they had been twenty-four hours earlier. Voices were louder, telephones were ringing more incessantly, few of the precious chairs were occupied; the command post was vibrating with a cacophonous discord.

There were still three distinct camps: the politicians who wanted to appease the terrorists, regardless of cost; the National Police, who were emphatically unwilling to give in to extortion, again almost regardless of cost; and the scientists who were thoroughly convinced that explosive disablement was both safe and the only logical solution to the problem.

The debate had evolved to the point where an outside observer might conclude that everyone involved in the discussion felt it more important to win the argument than to choose the right course. Shouting and arm waving were the preferred method of communication, and rational discussion was becoming scarcer by the moment.

The negotiations with the terrorists did seem to be progressing, their demands having been altered to the release of the three prisoners, fifty million francs, a public apology for unspecified grievances against the French Muslim community, and assurances that Muslim applicants would have preference in future French Civil Service appointments. The prime minister, who seemed to be favoring this camp, had already agreed to deliver the desired apology in a news conference later that evening.

It was probably fortunate that the six men at Ground Zero had no idea of what was happening at the command post. As they sat waiting for directions, their anxiety was growing as the silent vigil continued. Pierre's attempt to break the tension with "If things go wrong, at least our families won't have to pay for coffins" did not elicit a single murmur. The terrorists' threat letter had promised that nothing would happen for another two hours—at this point, another hour and fifty-two minutes, to be exact—but it was increasingly hard to take much solace in that.

"Bise, Bise"—the radio had crackled fifteen minutes earlier. "Are you ready?"

"We will be in just a few minutes. Do you have a decision?"

"Just hold tight, I think they're almost there."

Then no response, nothing but silence. So all they could do was wait some more, each wrapped in his own thoughts, taking no solace at all in the knowledge that, if something happened, their bones would be interned in perpetuity with those of Robespierre and Marie Antoinette.

Pierre slipped over to sit beside Bison. "Bise, why don't we just foam and go? I don't believe that we're high on the decision makers' list of concerns. Politically, they've got nothing to lose: if that thing fails to detonate, they become heroes; if it does go off, the story is that the team of brave, deceased scientists set it off while attempting to render it safe. We're dispensable; if you look at it that way, we're nothing more than convenient pawns."

While Bise would not admit it, he had entertained similar thoughts. He was reluctant to follow Pierre's suggestion because the foam had such a limited lifetime. If they foamed now and left, there would be little protection by 5:00 pm: even if only the chemical explosive detonated, it would probably be enough energy to vent through the top of the cavern. As scientific commander, it was his responsibility to balance the risk of his team's safety with the need to protect the city. He was aware that his men were watching him, all ready to leave, all waiting for some signal from him to do so. He suddenly realized how honored he was by the confidence they—especially the two French technicians he had met only two days ago—were demonstrating in his leadership. No, it was not yet time to go.

The radio issued another random series of blips and then again went silent. The men looked expectantly at one another but remained quiet. Could the radio have failed? Could the command post be trying to contact them? No way of knowing, but they should have considered the possibility of communication breakdown earlier. Each returned to their increasingly anxious thoughts, and, while listening to the cavern "music" as the draft whistled through its collection of all of those human remains, each silently cursed the people upstairs whose principal interests they feared were too highly influenced by their own political futures.

The radio clicked again, breaking the reverie. Just static, nothing more. Finally, wanting to ask no more of his colleagues, Bison picked up the radio.

"Admiral, this is Bise. What's going on?" No answer.

"Is there anyone there"? Still nothing.

The wait resumed, now worse, interrupted occasionally by the sound of bones shifting, probably triggered by some resident rat looking for a better vantage point. By the time Alan broke the silence by reporting that it was getting close to going-to-work-time back home, a cloud of gloom pervaded the cavern.

Everyone sat without speaking, deep in personal thought, five minutes seeming like hours and ten minutes an eternity. There was nothing any of them wanted to do more than just to get out of there; the thing that kept them there was their loyalty and respect for Bison. They all recognized that even here there was a limit; if someone decided he could no longer continue and opted to leave, everyone would probably follow. Loyalty and respect have their limits and can become hazy in the face of imminent death.

All six heads snapped to full alert as a rapid series of grinding noises came from somewhere within the device, these ominous sounds followed immediately by a highly distinct snap.

They had all heard that snap before; it was the unique sound made by the closure of a mechanical relay. While frightening, it was in some respects a welcome sound: now something had to happen. No one questioned why, in this day of sophisticated electronic switching, the device might contain such ancient technology as a mechanical relay. It really didn't matter; to a man they all surmised that the sound signified the beginning of a countdown sequence.

Bison's "That's it, we're out of here!" caused everyone to swing into action. They all knew their prescribed tasks, but Bison repeated them aloud to be sure. He was somewhat concerned that the foam would have to stand for almost an hour if the 5:00 pm time was real. But there was nothing that could be done about that. Besides, he rationalized, if the disablement was successful, they were dealing with only about twenty pounds of explosive, and even the skeleton foam might be able to handle that.

As he looked around, Alan and Michel had already finished their assignments and were leaving. Paul and Henri had the foam machines churning, high pressure water driving the fans and throwing the water and the educted surfactant against the mesh screen at the front of the machine and making beautiful, white fluffy foam. They glanced at him for his approval, received it, and began moving toward the exit. Pierre, after confirming that the diagnostic box was functioning properly and pulling the cord to open the air vent on the top of the cone, was right on their heels. Bison waited until the cone was nearly half-filled and, when he was convinced everything was operating correctly, ran over, inserted and turned the key that actuated the firing set, and then hustled to the exit, exhibiting the run that Jean Denis had once referred to as the Bison waddle.

Ten minutes later, a breathless Bison emerged from the tunnel into the quarry, where he was met by the other members of his Working Point team, Jean Denis, and a group of policemen and technicians. His heart still pumping at one hundred and forty beats a minute or so, he was filled with a once-in-a-lifetime rush of adrenaline—this one far surpassing the thrill of kicking the winning field goal that he had envisioned so many years ago. Looking around, he sensed that everyone there, especially the other members of his band of six, was similarly pumped. The adrenaline was at such a level that no one needed to speak: just looking at their compatriots was sufficient to express their gratitude at being outside in the sunshine and to express their affection to their brothers.

The police were erecting a makeshift closure over the tunnel exit when the telephone from the command post rang. "Bison," an excited Giles shouted, "get out of there now! Somehow the police have been forced to capitulate; they've reached some kind of agreement with the terrorists. So get your team out of there as fast as you can because it's less than an hour before the deadline and most of us up here have little trust in what's going to happen next. Do you hear me, Bison?"

"Yes, Giles, we're already outside in the quarry. Something in the device clicked, and we're convinced that it started some kind of countdown phase. So we set up the disablement charge, foamed, and left the Innocents chamber about fifteen minutes ago. My guess is that the terrorists couldn't turn it off now if they wanted to. I'm heading back to the States immediately, and the rest of the group down here should be up at the prefecture within about ten or fifteen minutes. Tell the admiral I'll see him back home."

"I can't express how grateful we are to you, Bise, thank you," the prefect said, which was followed by the admiral's voice: "Thank you, Bise, and come back to Washington and see me as soon as everything gets quieted down."

"Will do. Bye." Setting the receiver down, Bison turned back to Jean Denis. "I'll bet you a bottle of your overpriced wine that they can't stop it now. I'm not sure what it was we heard, but there was definitely something going on inside that weapon. Let's get the hell out of here."

Jean Denis picked up some of Bison's personal gear as they headed for Bison's police escort to the airport. When they got there, a visibly emotional Jean Denis turned to Bison. "I hope I don't need to tell you how grateful I am. No matter how this turns out, both France and I owe you more than we can ever repay. Give the Princess an extra hug for me and tell her we look forward to meeting her lucky new husband when we come across to the States next spring."

Within five minutes, the quarry area was deserted. The traffic, despite the almost constant blare of sirens, was moving surprisingly well on the surface streets.

•   •   •

Arriving at the command post, Jean Denis, Pierre, and the rest of the response team sensed a divisiveness and anger far greater than expected. They personally were met with gratitude but not much joy. The nonpolitical camp was extremely angry over the appeasement decision agreed to by the prime minister. The victors in the debate were obviously pleased, but they were still busy attempting to prove to the terrorists that they could uphold their side of the bargain. All of the paperwork required to make the monetary transfer had been started; it was uncertain if the actual transfer had been accomplished, but it was imminent. Two of the prisoners were in France and the third would soon leave Denver for Paris. The prime minister had requested time on television to address the French people at 6:00 PM, planning to apologize for the past mistreatment of the Muslims by previous French governments. Finally, the prime minister had already ordered that a special committee be established to determine how to give the Muslim population preferential treatment in securing government employment.

In the last discussion with the terrorists, an agreement had been reached to extend the deadline until 10:00 am the next morning. By then, all three prisoners would be out of US custody, the monetary transfer would be complete, and the terrorists would have ascertained if the prime minister's speech had properly addressed their grievances. The prime minister was on the phone with a representative of the US secretary of state attempting to resolve the final issues of the release of the prisoner in Denver when one of the mayor's minions grabbed his arm and whispered something in his ear.

"What?" the prime minister yelled angrily, passing the phone to one of his subordinates and grabbing a piece of paper handed to him by the messenger. As he reread the message, the prime minister's face turned crimson. He turned, obviously enraged and yelling emphatically to get the attention of the rest of the room. "I need your attention! I mean right now! I have just been handed a message which I assume comes from the terrorists, is that correct?" he asked, looking at the cowering messenger. Receiving an affirmative head nod, he read the message aloud.

"We're sorry but it is too late, we no longer can control the weapon. Inshallah."

A hush crept over the entire gathering as each individual tried to absorb this information and determine what to do. Almost immediately, the prime minister, turning toward the prefect, shouted, "Throw that damned disablement switch!"

"Yes, sir!" responded the prefect, throwing up the switch guard covering the Fire button.

CHAPTER SEVEN
Bison
Wednesday, September 13, 1995
5:00 pm

Even though the traffic lessened as the police car made its way out of the Latin Quarter toward Charles de Gaulle airport, Bison was becoming more impatient with every breath. He glanced toward the direction of Ground Zero and then down at his watch. He repeated this motion so many times that the observing driver inquired, "Sir, are you worried about missing your plane? What time is it due to leave?"

Sheepishly, Bison admitted, "There's no hurry, we're just fine. We'll have plenty of time as long as we don't encounter any major holdups."

"Then please, sir, trust me and just sit back and relax. I'll get you there in plenty of time for your flight. You may even have time to go to Brasserie Flo in Terminal 2F and have a bottle or two of our fine wine. Don't worry."

Bison acknowledged the suggestion with a smile, refrained from looking at his watch for the rest of the trip but did, several times, cast a furtive glance back toward the Latin Quarter. The sight of the Latin Quarter that was running through his mind was not the lively, carefree setting of yesterday's restaurants with laughter and gardens; that happy place had been replaced by the vision of a shattered, rubble-strewn aftermath of a nuclear detonation. Sitting in the back seat of the speeding police car all alone with his thoughts, Bison bowed his head and prayed.

Arriving at the airport, Bison thanked his driver, picked up his luggage, and hustled inside. Only then did he permit himself to look at a clock; when he did, it read 5:30. The deadline was long passed. Surely if there'd been a nuclear detonation, he would have heard it. He was elated; assuming that the timer in the weapon was accurate, either their disablement had worked or the weapon had fizzled of its own accord.

"Thank God. It's over, it's over, I think it's all over," Bison exalted, somewhat louder than he had planned as he reached for his cell phone. Several of his fellow travelers stole a glance at him, no doubt thinking here was just another dirty, disheveled, unshaven loud foreigner, probably an American, who had consumed too much wine. As he stood there in the middle of the concourse waiting for Jean Denis's ringing phone to be answered, Bison felt the adrenaline-induced energy draining from his body, his weary legs suddenly feeling as if they were no longer up to the task of supporting his body. He found a chair and, as the phone continued to ring, he suddenly realized that, with everything else that was going on, neither Jean Denis nor anyone else at the command post was going to be taking phone calls.

His filthy appearance sentenced him to an extraordinarily prolonged interrogation by a hostile customs agent who found it necessary to examine his passport with unusual attention and to ask a multitude of questions regarding how he enjoyed his stay in France. When he was released to go up to the departure area, he didn't even bother browsing the duty free shops for a present for Bev; all he wanted was something to eat and a drink, and, once on board, a peaceful nap throughout the long flight home.

But first he'd like to get some confirmation from Jean Denis. After yet another unsuccessful attempt, he realized that Jean Denis would, if things had gone as planned, right now be leading the recovery team back into the catacombs to confirm their success—no wonder he could not answer his phone.

When he entered the Admirals Club, everyone was huddled around the various television sets, chattering excitedly. Working his way forward so he could hear, Bison's limited French allowed him to understand that the animated reporter was discussing an explosion that occurred late that afternoon in the Fourth Arrondissement, in an area that had been evacuated earlier in the day due to a chlorine leak.

When the news conference was interrupted for a commercial break, Bison asked the somber gentleman next to him if he spoke English. When the man allowed that he did, Bison asked what was going on. Looking over Bison and his untidiness exceedingly carefully, the gentleman finally deigned to answer the impertinent American. "There's been some kind of a chlorine explosion in the catacombs. The reporter seemed to feel that it might have been caused by a terrorist but the police seem unwilling to confirm anything."

Despite what seemed like good news, Bison still could not completely shake his black cloud of fear. He took his combination of hopefulness and apprehensiveness into the McDonald's and emerged fifteen minutes later with a Big Mac, eating it on his rush to the boarding lounge.

The crowds surrounding the TVs in the concourse lounge were now four to five people deep, and they all seemed completely entranced and even more engaged than previously. When he finally got close enough to see the screen, there was the prime minister, the prefect, and the mayor of Paris, all smiles and all talking at the same time—the mayor managing to talk over the other two. Bison was able to understand enough to know that they were now talking about a thwarted nuclear terrorist event, and he caught the word "catacombs."

"That is really frightening!" the young man, possibly a university student, standing next to Bison said in English.

Turning toward him, Bison replied "I'm afraid I didn't catch it all. What's going on?"

"There's been another terrorist event. Someone planted a nuclear weapon in the catacombs over in the Fourth Arrondissement. It apparently was scheduled to detonate about 5:00 pm this afternoon but the police and the government's response team managed to destroy it before it went off. There's a huge mess in the catacombs but they pretty much managed to contain it there. Surprisingly enough, our French government was really prepared." The young man anxiously turned his attention back to the TV where the news conference was continuing.

The American standing there in the midst of the proud French crowd was positively jubilant. He had not realized how much tension he'd been carrying, how tightly wound with fear he had been. The more he observed the relief of the individuals on the TV screen, the more he was able to relax. Reluctantly turning away from the TV, he walked through the tunnel to the overseas boarding lounges. Here again, all of his fellow travelers were huddled around the television. The news conference was over but the interest and concern regarding the nuclear incident was still at a high level. At the moment, the news correspondents were interviewing some French bureaucrat, apparently from the prime minister's office, an individual Bison didn't recognize. The official seemed to be saying that all of the danger was over but that people should wait until further notice before returning to their homes and offices. Over and over, the commentator praised the work of the police, the French military, government officials, the mayor's office, and the scientists from the CEA. He failed to catch any acknowledgement of the support from the United States; he understood that national pride and potential political ramifications quite possibly prevented recognizing his team's help, and found that he was even able to smile when he imagined Jean Denis's apoplectic reaction to the oversight.

He listened a bit longer to see if they interviewed anyone he recognized. Reluctantly, he gave up and shortly before 7:00 pm he boarded his flight for the long ride home, hoping that somehow he would be rested well enough and mentally rejuvenated to enjoy and participate properly in the glorious weekend that was before him.

CHAPTER EIGHT
Jean Denis
Wednesday, September 13, 1995
4:30 pm

The team he left behind just outside the catacombs was not offered that same respite from the continuing tension. It was nearly 4:30 pm by the time they made it back to command center. Everyone in the room, except those closely following the ongoing discussion between the negotiators and the terrorists, descended upon them en masse. While a sense of relief existed because of the agreement that had been reached with the terrorists, few of them believed that the problem had been completely resolved, and they all seemed to need questions answered about what had occurred at Ground Zero.

Finally, Giles and the admiral managed to establish some order, and Pierre was able to describe the sequence of events.

"We were all sitting there, scared as hell, but all we could do was sit. The disablement charge had been set up, the cone was totally air-inflated, and the foam generators were hooked up and ready to go. We would have left then, except we were worried about the limited lifetime of the foam. No one had anything to say and the quiet made the tension worse. I suspect that there was a lot of praying going on, even by skeptics like myself. I promise you, I've never been in a situation like that, not even close. I was scared. It was even worse because we seemed to have lost communication with you, we didn't know what was going on, and we were getting angrier by the minute. I told Bison a couple of times that we should foam and get the hell out of there, but there was no way he would leave. And if he stayed, we stayed. So there we sat for what seemed like an eternity, staring at that damned weapon.

"All of a sudden, shortly after 4:00 pm, something happened inside that crate. All of us recognized that sound. It was the distinctive click of a large mechanical relay snapping shut. It seemed to echo back and forth through the chamber forever, almost like the terrorists were taunting us. We didn't know what the relay started, but whatever it was, we knew we needed to get out of there. Bison hollered 'That's it' or something like that. Michel and Alan made a last check of the alignment of the shaped charge, Paul and Henri opened the water valves to start the foaming, I checked on the diagnostics box, and Bison turned on the firing set and made sure that the cone was filling properly with foam. Then we all got out of there. I was so scared that I even beat Bison to the door. Oh, and I'd like to add one other thing: I've never seen such courage and camaraderie in all my life. There was no whimpering, no whining. I, for one, would be willing to follow Bison Baird wherever he asked me to go."

As soon as Pierre finished, questions filled the air. "Is the device armed now?" "Were there any other noises from the box after the relay closed?" "Are you still convinced that the noise was really a relay?" "Wouldn't it have been better if you had waited for a decision from up here?"

He was just beginning to try and figure out a diplomatic way to explain the facts of life to the last questioner when the prime minister's frantic command to "Throw that damned disablement switch!" filled the room with instant terror.

Everything went silent, absolutely dead silent. But only for a matter of seconds. Almost immediately, there was a slight tremor, and the overhead lights began to sway. The indicators on the diagnostic box illuminated, signaling both an increase in radioactive level in the chamber and the presence of a significant transient pressure pulse. All of the phones in the operations center began to ring. One of the calls was from the local seismologic station, reporting the detection of an unusual pressure pulse, one whose wave shape was distinctly different from that of an earthquake.

The entire assemblage looked expectantly at Giles. "May I have your attention please?" he responded. "What we have just witnessed is exactly what would be expected if our disablement attempt has been successful, if the chemical explosive has detonated without initiating any type of nuclear event. If that is true, we have been very lucky and the most fearful part of this potential disaster is over."

Raising his voice to a near-shout in order to be heard over the celebratory din that erupted, he continued. "We do, however, need to be cautious in proclaiming success just yet. We need to get eyewitness confirmation that the device has been destroyed before we can be unequivocally positive that we've been successful. I would highly advise that the public not be informed of our probable success until we have that confirmation. If we have been successful, much of the catacombs are now filled with a thick cloud of broken-down foam, dust, and airborne radioactive particulate. We expect most of this to settle out rapidly. I have asked Jean Denis to lead the recovery team, and they are shortly going to be suiting up with SCUBA gear to go into the chamber. By far, their most urgent task is to confirm that the weapon no longer exists. But that's not their only assignment. We suspect that there still is a several kilogram ball of plutonium somewhere in that mess; we need to recover that to avert the possibility of someone else finding it and attempting to use it again. We also wish to try and recover the US firing set. Finally, we'd like to have them pick up any remnants of the destroyed weapon, particularly that relay and timer, that they can in the off chance we can get enough information to understand exactly what we were facing. Jean Denis and his crew will not attempt any cleanup of the site; I'm afraid that that is probably a chore for many decontamination experts over the next several months."

•   •   •

Jean Denis and his five-man recovery team entered the underground by the door on Rue Remy Dumoncel. As soon as the door was open, their instruments detected elevated levels of radioactive particulate. "We have airborne radiation." Jean Denis spoke into the communication system that tied all of them together. The closer they got to the Cemetery of the Innocents, the thicker the cloud of dust and particulate became. As they rounded the horseshoe curve in the tunnel and reached the Crypt of Passion, they began to observe the chaos that had been created.

The formerly neatly stacked bones of the ancient Parisians were flung everywhere, all covered with carbon-laden decomposed foam. Dark, syrupy water was running down the cavern floor, making walking in the decontamination suits even more hazardous. The blast had badly scarred the surface of the walls near where the device had been, but the walls themselves, although extensively carved by flying shrapnel, were still intact. And, more importantly, the ceiling above the device was also still in place, although it now possessed a decided concavity.

Jean Denis, in the lead, fought his way through the mess to Ground Zero. There was a cavity about half a meter deep and a meter across in the floor where the device had been, but few remnants of the device itself; without question, the device had been destroyed.

"Commo link, Commo link," he yelled into his microphone, "do you copy?"

"Go ahead, Jean Denis, we hear," came back.

"Tell Giles that the device no longer exists. We're absolutely positive. Did you get that?"

"Yes, Jean Denis. Tell Giles that the weapon has been destroyed, is that correct?"

"That is correct. And tell the relief crew to prepare to come in, as we're not going to have enough oxygen to stay here too much longer."

"Will do."

They found the disablement firing set quickly. It was nearly severed in two, having suffered both a direct hit from a large fragment of the steel casing of the artillery shell and a series of less-serious impacts from flying femurs and tibias. They picked up several unidentifiable metallic objects, all heavily damaged, before Jean Denis signaled that it was time to leave because of their dwindling oxygen supply.

"Hey, Giles," Jean Denis reported by phone as soon as they were out in the open air and free of the SCUBA masks. "It's all clear down there. There are essentially no remnants of the weapon. We haven't seen anything that tells us whether it was our disablement system or their firing set that set the device off. It appears that there was no nuclear reaction; we couldn't pick up any fission fragment signatures. We did find the disablement system firing set and several weapon components that we haven't yet been able to identify. Unfortunately, we haven't located the plutonium sphere; we're probably going to have to bring better detectors down here to find it—this is an unbelievable mess. But I have no reservations about declaring the operation a success and releasing that information to the public."

•   •   •

It took until Friday morning and several more rotations of personnel into the chamber before the plutonium sphere was finally located, buried in rubble more than ten meters from its origin. The sphere showed evidence of melting on its surface, undoubtedly a consequence of its compression heating by the HE; this would be the source of the airborne plutonium particulate they had detected. There were also several deep cavities on its outer surface; probably corrosion effects. While members of the recovery team were not weapons experts, they all agreed that if the weapon had gone nuclear, it probably would have been a much-reduced yield. The plutonium sphere, the US firing set, and all of the recovered weapon components were turned over to Jean Denis to be sent to the CEA laboratory in Bordeaux for further analysis.

The debate over how to clean up the mess began almost instantaneously. The radioactive danger was now from the suspended particulate, and since plutonium has a long half-life, the problem would not take care of itself naturally. While the airborne material would settle out with time, the problem then was resuspension. Any activity in the chambers would disrupt the settled-out material and reinitiate the problem. Therefore it was obvious to all but the most optimistic proponents that it would be necessary to spray something onto the cavities' surfaces to preclude this resuspension before the catacombs could again became a viable tourist attraction.

From how Jean Denis had described the chamber's state, it was clear that it was going to take a Herculean effort to reassemble all of the scattered bones. The mayor's staff started campaigning Friday morning to start the recovery operation the following day. The police and Jean Denis opposed this plan since all of the device's remnants had not yet been located and there could be pieces of unexploded explosive hidden in the mess. By Sunday afternoon, the police were still not prepared to assent to the cleanup operation; they wanted to be sure that everything was done safely and methodically, and that all the physical evidence was recovered.

Ever since the first communiqué from the terrorists, the national police had tried to find the source of the messages. They were ultimately unsuccessful. They did trace some of the communications to a group of computers stolen from a secondary school in the Muslim section of the city, but were unable to locate the senders of the messages, and were met with a complete lack of cooperation from people in the neighborhood. There were no further leads, and, after the message from the terrorists that informed the officials that they no longer had control of the device, the terrorist contingent simply disappeared.

CHAPTER NINE
Bison
Wednesday September 13, 1995
7:00 pm

Bison had experienced many pleasant and comfortable trans-Atlantic trips. This was not one of them. He was in the upstairs lounge of a 747, the service was attentive, and the surroundings were pleasant. But he could not turn off his racing mind.

He replayed the last three days over and over. Each time he came to the same inescapable conclusion: they had been very, very lucky. The terrorists' timer could easily have been inaccurate and the device could have detonated while they were sitting in the cavern. And just what was that noise they had heard—was it really a mechanical relay? That was almost unbelievable. Why would anyone incorporate an archaic relay in a modern, sophisticated firing system? With these thoughts continuing to race through his mind, he attempted to sleep.

After several hours of squirming and turning, he turned on his overhead light. His was the only one that was on in the cabin; everyone else appeared to have found sleep. He checked his watch expectantly, but they were still several hours out of JFK. He punched his light off, rearranged his body, and willed himself to sleep.

As the obsessive thoughts about the hours in the catacombs descended once again, he examined, for the first time, his own actions. Why? Why had he and the others so readily accepted the risk of their own demise in an effort to solve a problem for which they really had no responsibility? He did not think the answer was peer pressure or testosterone; neither of those possibilities

135

seemed to him to be strong enough provocations to accept that degree of risk. No, he felt that it had to be something deeper, something inherent in the human soul that would lead him and others to such actions. Perhaps it was the same inherent humanity that would cause a bystander who couldn't swim to jump into water to save a drowning infant. Bison had long believed that God had infused every human's soul with a sense of responsibility for other humans, particularly for those who were less able to care for themselves. Maybe this was just another manifestation of that responsibility. But that left him with a major philosophical dilemma: how then could he explain the motives of the terrorists who believed in the same God as Bison but who had left the bomb in the catacombs and were willing, perhaps even anxious, to kill thousands of their fellow human beings simply because they adhered to the teachings of a different prophet? Would these perpetrators jump into the pool to save a drowning Islamic baby? Or a Christian baby? He wanted to believe that the answer was yes, but he was at a loss to explain the incongruity. Perhaps his premise could still be valid if he accepted that the indoctrination the terrorists underwent was strong enough to override the fundamental sense of humanity—that they believed that the promised ends justified the brutal means. He found this answer somewhat plausible but not altogether satisfactory as he, yet again, shifted around in his seat trying to get comfortable. This new positioning of his legs turned out to be the magical one; he was soundly asleep when the wheels of the plane lowered for the landing in New York.

The anticipation of seeing Bev and the Princess compensated for the short five hours of sleep he managed at the JFK Holiday Inn before his early morning flight back home. He glanced at the headlines in the papers as he passed the news racks on his way into breakfast. "Nuclear Threat in Paris," "Nuclear Artillery Shell in Catacombs," "A Triumph for French Science" with the subtitle "Could the US Do As Well?" were the headlines that blared at the passerby. As he drank his coffee and enjoyed his bacon and eggs, he overheard segments of conversation from the patrons around him; all of the discussion seemed to be about the problem in Paris. When he left the coffee shop, Bison refrained from purchasing any of the newspapers; he was not yet prepared to rekindle that experience.

He arrived back in Albuquerque right on schedule. As exhilarated as he was to see his girls when they picked him up, all he could come up with was "long and very tiring" to the inevitable, "How was your trip?"

Both Bev and the Princess knew where he had been and why. They had heard about the successful outcome on the news but had no idea of the extent of his participation; all the news reports were heralding the efforts of the French police and scientists. Even "Did you see Jean Denis?" generated only a "Yes, Christine is pregnant again, they're all doing just fine and are still planning on coming over late in the spring."

He did manage to get a short nap and shower before crawling into his tux for the wedding rehearsal and rehearsal dinner. Most of their close friends knew that "Bison had been out of town again," but no one knew where he'd been or why. Following the ground rules that had been established long ago, no one asked.

The wedding the next evening was beautiful. The bride was beautiful, the mother-of-the-bride was beautiful, and dad was just very relieved. In the back of his mind, though, Bison could not stop dreading the inevitable replaying, second-guessing, and possible recriminations he knew he would face when he went back to work on Monday morning.

•   •   •

The phone rang fifteen minutes after Bison sat down at his desk on Monday morning. *"What took them so long?"* he murmured to himself. He was wrong; the person on the other end did not want to interrogate him.

"Guess what we found?" Jean Denis demanded, not identifying himself and not waiting for an answer. "We've found the timer from the weapon's firing system. We're sure of it. It had been activated and it had started timing down. There were thirteen minutes left when the blast hit it and pretty well destroyed it. You know what that means? You were right, that thing was timing down! And our disablement charge destroyed it! What's more, we chose the right spot to hit with the shaped charge. I couldn't wait to tell you. We found it on Friday, but Christine threatened me if I interfered with the wedding. I'm so proud of you, my friend, just think of what we've done. You ought to be excited because there are at least a half-dozen people, some of whom I'd bet that you've never met, walking around here taking credit for what you did, saying that they argued all along for the disablement option and some actually claim that they helped in its design.

"I can't talk long, Pierre's on his way back with more pieces and Giles wants to review our progress; we're still finding parts of the device hidden in all of that muck that you made." Jean Denis was now talking so fast that he was almost breathless. "We've been going at it slowly because I want either Pierre or myself to be there all the time, at least until we think we have found everything of significance; that pit was in pretty sad shape. I don't know if I've mentioned it or not, but we did find your battered firing set; I'm assuming you'd like it back."

"Bise, I want you to know that without your insight on the one-point safety question, I'm not sure that the prefect would have had the guts to risk firing the disablement charge even after the terrorists lost control. I can't tell you how indebted the French people are to you. Pierre's here so I need to run, but I'll get back to you shortly."

With that, Jean Denis hung up, barely giving Bison a chance to say goodbye and thank him for the kind words. Jean Denis had been so excited that he hadn't even asked about the wedding—he'd have to answer to Christine for that.

Bison found himself having trouble tackling the work that had piled up on his desk in his absence. It didn't help that it seemed as if the whole organization wanted to talk to him about his experiences and that he found he was relishing the frequent interruptions. Everyone wanted their individual replay, some because they believed that new or revised policies might be required, a few to argue that his actions might have "stepped over the boundaries," but most simply wanted to share vicariously in his experience. Despite all the excitement, his lack of noticeable progress on formulating the upcoming project review was beginning to make him question his decision to come into work. He had considered taking a few days vacation; he could just as well prepare the review at home. Then he thought about other members of his team returning to work, and it didn't seem fair that they should be put through the ordeal of justifying everything that had taken place by themselves. Reflection on that justification forced him to laugh at himself; he was enjoying the hell out of the replaying.

Try as he might, he could not get his mind off Paris. He considered calling Jean Denis a dozen times that day but knew his friend would be swamped. When the phone rang as soon as he got to work the next morning, he was delighted to hear a French voice. Jean Denis was pumped by what they were finding and had new information that he wanted to share but, restraining himself, he took the time to exchange pleasantries and to ask about the Princess and her wedding. "Yes," he admitted, "Christine had sort of mentioned my negligence."

Finally, preliminaries satisfied, they got down to the point of the call. Jean Denis said that it was his belief that they had recovered about everything that they were going to find in the catacombs and that it was going to take much longer than they originally estimated to restore the tourist attraction.

"It's an unbelievable mess down there. We were really relieved when we finally found the plutonium pit. We also found several pieces of what we believe were the device's control system among all that muck and grime. We were right, those were NiCad batteries that we saw on the X-rays, but we still haven't figured out how the system was supposed to work nor do we know why they thought that they needed all of that power. We have found nothing to change our conclusion that it was our disablement charge and not their firing system that set off the explosive. With no nuclear yield! That is so damned amazing that I still can't believe it."

When Jean Denis slowed to take a breath, Bison was able to ask, "How about the relay? Have you found anything like that?"

"Negative, nothing at all like that. But we have found lots of small pieces of components that we haven't been able to identify. While Pierre has a different explanation almost every day for what was happening with the device during those last few minutes, we're all still in agreement with your conclusion that the system was in countdown mode. There's no question that it was the right call to get out of there when you did."

The conversation ended shortly thereafter, with Jean Denis reconfirming his and Christine's upcoming visit.

The rest of the day was one of the most pleasant of Bison's entire lifetime; he was exhilarated by the confirmation that his judgments regarding making the final preparations for disablement and abandoning the Working Point had been correct. The nightmare resulting from the possibility that he had made a cowardly decision could now be permanently retired.

CHAPTER TEN
Bison, 1996

The phone call from the admiral came several months later, shortly after the first of the year. "Bison, I just got a call from the French Embassy, and they want to present us with their Legion of Honour for our assistance last fall. It will be a rather formal affair on February 18; you know how elaborately the French do those things. I would like you and Bev to attend as our guests. They've requested that we keep our party small so it will just be the two of you, me and my wife, one of my staff from here, and someone from the Nevada Field Office—no, don't worry, not PJ. I will let you know the details as soon as they're firmed up, but I'd be most pleased if you can join us."

"I can't tell you how honored I am. Of course we'll be there. Thank you so much for the invitation," Bison responded. As he hung up the phone, he hoped that whatever else might be on his and Bev's calendar could be postponed; this was certainly a once-in-a-lifetime event.

He managed to wait until Bev came home from work that evening to tell her; he wanted to tell her in person so he could observe firsthand her excitement and the little giggle that he loved so much. He knew that this would be followed almost immediately by the delightful, "What shall I wear? I don't have anything to wear! I need to go shopping!" exuberance he had grown to love so long ago.

• • •

The admiral was right. The reception in the historic Élysée Palace was by far the most elegant, most imposing affair Bison had ever attended. He was so pleased that Bev had had the chance to enjoy it with him; she had been a bit down since the Princess was no longer at home and no longer in frequent need of her advice.

When the admiral's wife and the hugely pregnant Christine escorted Bev off to tour the grand palace after the ceremony, the prefect, Jean Denis, the admiral, and Bison were standing in a group with just-refilled glasses of Champagne when the prefect remarked offhandedly, "Bison, Jean Denis and I discussed this just last week and, you know, there is something that we still don't understand about what happened that afternoon in the catacombs. Perhaps you can explain. As I flipped up the safety guard on the firing set, we felt the tremble from the HE detonation just a split second before I'd managed to activate the fire button. Honestly, I never got a chance to throw that switch."

"What? How could that happen?" Bison spontaneously responded, surreptitiously looking at Jean Denis's face and finding the conspiratorial grin that he had halfway expected.

Then the prefect said two words Bison never would have anticipated and would always remember: "Thank you."

They knew. The prefect, Jean Denis, and the admiral knew. Not only did they understand that Bison had set in motion the circuitry to fire the disablement charge, they had just acknowledged approval of his action. The prefect had forgiven him for committing the unforgivable leadership sin: making a decision that was not his to make.

It had been a premeditated decision. During the long, solemn wait in the cavern, he had absolutely convinced himself that that weapon would not produce a nuclear yield with a single-point initiation. He had decided that there were circumstances under which he felt it was honorable to take it upon himself to activate the disablement charge. That relay closure and what they all perceived to be the start of the weapon countdown sequence satisfied these self-imposed conditions. In all of the commotion of their hurried exit, when Bison rushed back to activate the firing set, he also activated the manual override firing sequence to fire the shaped charge prior to the 5:00 pm deadline, giving the team sufficient time to get out of the catacombs. Even though everything had turned out beautifully, he was still haunted by his usurpation of authority, and it had been his hope during the intervening months that no one would ever find out that he had violated the trust they had invested in him.

But these three men knew and had lauded his action. And their demeanor indicated that no one else would ever know. No one else ever did.

Inshallah indeed.

EPILOGUE

Three worlds, three cultures, three ideologies, all answering what they felt was their call, all culminating that September afternoon in the Parisian catacombs. While each individual followed his or her conscience, each grew to question what previously had been unassailable convictions.

Evgeny found that as much as he cherished his homeland and the people of the Chelyabinsk, he treasured the love and welfare of his family more. Mose, Masud, and Minifu began to realize, after living in the world of the infidels and without their mentors' constant radical thought reinforcement, that perhaps it actually was not Allah's desire that all nonbelievers should perish. And Bison was surprised to find that he was capable of overstepping his authority, something he could not previously have imagined doing. Were these acts of dedication? Most certainly. Of courage? Without a doubt. But there was a certainly a trace of cowardice and self-interest in all of them.

Life, of course, continued after that Wednesday afternoon. Lilia, with Dmitry's help and after tedious arbitration, was able to collect on Evgeny's insurance policy and build a small home near her in-laws. The settlement provided her and her girls with enough money to enjoy a comfortable lifestyle.

Mose, Masud, and Minifu all returned from Paris to their camp in Northern Sudan. Masud and Minifu quickly discovered that they no longer possessed the zeal for "the cause" and, after much deliberation and soul searching, were permitted to return to Cairo where Masud had a joyful reunion with his parents. Both he and Minifu found fulfilling jobs with the Egyptian Museum where, a few years later, they were surprised by a visit from their old colleague, Mose, who was on his way to the terrorist camps in Afghanistan.

As the years went by, Bison found that his job became even more loaded with administrative tasks (many of which he felt were of questionable merit) and devoid of the problem-solving he loved. As soon as they were financially able, he and Bev moved to a small acreage in the South of France where Bison found immense pleasure in nurturing a few scraggly grape vines and a herd of scruffy goats. There were no bureaucrats in sight.

ABOUT THE AUTHORS

His 38-year career at Sandia National Laboratories in Albuquerque placed Bill Hartman near the center of many of the country's nuclear weapon programs, stretching from the Eisenhower era into the Clinton years. He personally developed much of the analysis to permit assessing the risk of transporting nuclear weapons within the US, led the program to develop aqueous foam for the containment of high-explosive detonations, and managed a project to develop an air-droppable nuclear weapon effects simulator. He was twice the recipient of the coveted Nuclear Weapon Program's *Award of Excellence* and has published over twenty technical reports and articles covering everything from the spallation properties of 6061-T6 aluminum to involvement in President Carter's and the UN's attempt to define a proliferation-resistant nuclear fuel cycle. His last assignment prior to his retirement in 1995 was as program manager for Sandia's NEST (Nuclear Emergency Search Team) and as one of the senior scientific commanders for the NEST response team.

A life-long avid reader of both fiction and non-fiction, Bill has not-to-surprisingly always been interested in books dealing with nuclear terrorism. Having personally worked with so many of the key players and with the actual bureaucracies involved, he saw an opportunity to shed much-needed realism into the often-unrealistic literature. Resolution of problems like the one depicted in this book will depend on real soldiers and real scientists; individuals who have spent much of their careers preparing for such an eventuality while recognizing that there will be no super-human swooping in at the last minute to save the day.

Her previous incarnations as an architectural historian and a magazine editor made Terri Hartman an ideal co-author to bring her Dad's somewhat technical writing style to life. She is now the general manager of Liz's Antique

Hardware in Los Angeles, and her true purpose in life, she believes, lies if finishing one of her half-completed crafts projects and beating her husband at backgammon.

Bill currently lives north of Tucson, Arizona with his beloved wife Jean and their feisty Jack Russell terrier Wazoo. Terri and her husband Doc live in downtown Los Angeles.

CLOSING NOTES

Many of the situations described in this book are factual; the people however are all fictional. The environmental insult inflicted upon the people of the Southern Urals by the former Soviet Union is well-documented as is the description of the educational, social, and economic situation in Egypt early in the 1990s. The organization Takfir wa Hijra, also known as 'The People of the Cave" is real. It was founded by Sayyid Qutb who, at one time, was a student at the University of Northern Colorado. Additionally, the descriptions of the necropolis which underlies Paris and the science and weapon physics which are presented in the book are authentic; the portrayal of the response procedures (as of 1995, at least) and the predicted weapon effects are also realistic. Though an actual situation such as the one presented in this book has not occurred, I believe that, if it should, the interactions between the many involved participants could be very similar to those presented here.

BIBLIOGRAPHY

Cockburn, Andrew and Leslie. *One Point Safe*. New York: Bantam Doubleday Dell, 1997

DeGroot, Gerard. *The Bomb: A Life*. London: Random House, 2004

Glasstone, Samuel and Dolan, P. J., *The Effects of Nuclear Weapons*, U.S. Government Printing Office, Washington, D.C., 1977

Lamb, David. *The Arabs, Journey Beyond the Mirage*. New York: Vintage Books, 1987

Rhodes, Richard. *The Making of the Atomic Bomb*. New York: Simon and Schuster Adult, 1995

Richelson, Jeffrey. *Defusing Armageddon*. New York: W.W. Norton and Company, 2009

Sholokhov, Mikhail. *Harvest on the Don*. New York: Alfred A Knopf, 1961 (translation)

Wright, Lawrence. *The Looming Tower*. New York: Alfred A Knopf, 2006